The
Other
Side
of Air

ALSO BY JEANNE BRASELTON

A False Sense of Well Being

The
Other
Side
of Air

A NOVEL

JEANNE BRASELTON

with an Afterword by Kaye Gibbons

Ballantine Books • New York

JY LS

A Ballantine Books Trade Paperback Edition

Copyright © 2006 by the Estate of Jeanne Braselton
Afterword copyright © 2006 by Kaye Gibbons
Reading Group Guide copyright © 2006 by Random House, Inc.

Published in the United States by Ballantine Books, an imprint of The Random House Publishing Group, a division of Random House, Inc., New York.

BALLANTINE and colophon are registered trademarks of Random House, Inc.
READER'S CIRCLE and colophon are trademarks of Random House, Inc.

Library of Congress Cataloging-in-Publication Data
Braselton, Jeanne.
    The other side of air / Jeanne Braselton ; with an afterword by Kaye Gibbons.
        p.   cm.
    ISBN 0-345-44310-1
        I. Title.
PS3602.R38O86 2006
813.'6—dc22   2005057200

Printed in the United States of America

www.thereaderscircle.com

9 8 7 6 5 4 3 2 1

Designed by Helene Berinsky

FOR ALBERT BOYD BRASELTON...

"Friend of poets."
Guardian of my solitude.
For our true, great love.

AND FOR KAYE GIBBONS...

Both sister and mother in spirit.
Friend always.
For teaching me to "go and do."

The Other Side of Air

NOW THAT I HAVE DIED, I SEE ALL AND KNOW ALL, and there's nothing I can do about it. Before, the frustration would've been intolerable, but the instruction would've been the same—let things go from your hands, watch them land where they will and be glad, be decent and do your best, take care of those who love you, make your bed, do the nastiest job of the day first—no lessons that require divine revelation, you see, only common sense, nothing supernatural. Consider how jangled the world would be if our judgment from beyond continued to mean anything. Not to say that having the power to reach down into lives to lift burdens and simplify sticky situations wouldn't be thrilling. From all indications, though, it wouldn't be the best use of a brief allotment of time and imaginative longing to consider our leaving as anything other than a final journey. And take a tip—

memories are all we're capable of offering in the way of influence.

People who have loved us tend to leave the rooms we lie in committed to do more, see more, and so be able to die sometime in the distant future with more honor and fewer regrets than they believe we took with us. They can wonder so intently at the meaning of it all that an answer which may have been stranded inside them, abandoned, or atrophied from disuse will finally, suddenly, make itself heard. Despite their conviction that intimations of how to live better lives felt far too urgent and true to have arisen from any ordinary thing, lessons that matter always come on the heels of the simple act of remembering words and acts of love given to them by the person they've had to close the door on.

Mothers and wives are naturally inclined to notice large and small improvements individuals could be making in their lives, but it doesn't take death to prove the futility of trying to coordinate people to behave according to directions you prefer, or to believe what you know to be an indisputable truth. A living, even partially alert mother knows the limits of her ability to change a mind if she happens to have a grown child like mine who turns away from any evidence that his successes would be less impressive were it not for his parents' willingness to get up at dawn and work until dark. Specific memories of love, though, once they begin coming in through the grieving, are invariably dependable revelations, which can be trusted to finish transformations we weren't able to see completed.

Living in love for seventy-three years kept me immune to a great deal of frustration. From the instant in 1925 when the eight-year-old boy who would eventually be my husband squinted up from a mud hole he was stirring with a long stick on the long dirt road that passed by my house and his outside Rome, Georgia, adoration contained all the possibilities of freedom and trust. Our first conversation was chiefly made up of debate over why a new girl who'd just moved from Athens, a college town even small children learned to disparage, felt righteous enough to suggest that he was going to drive the stick up into his head if he continued to pick his dirty nose with it.

He said I seemed like a person who liked to dictate. "You look like them that like to try out to be the boss of somebody, but I got a mama, though she don't smile correcting."

"I always smile," I told him, "when I'm doing something I'm good at."

"The teachers don't give out lessons on the first day, but I bet you're going to make up some hard homework for all your doll babies soon as you get to the house."

I said, "I'm not saying, and you can't talk. I didn't see you at school."

"I don't get up of a morning, like some, studying school."

"You think you can turn out, playing in a filthy hole? You look like you'd be in my grade, unless you were left back. You been left back?"

"No," he said, "I'm the right age, covering from the fever

is all. I'll be over by there directly. Mama said I could go when I felt like it. I might feel like it tomorrow, I may not."

"You must be Ephraim," I said. "The teacher called out your name and marked you absent. People told her you'd had a temperature."

"I did," he said, "but not now."

"Then you ought to report tomorrow," I said. "You don't want to get off to the wrong start. Wouldn't you hate not to turn out? My father's the principal over by the military school, and before we left Athens, he said the public school I'd have to go to had people sixteen in the third grade. I saw a boy with a beard and a mustache playing tetherball today. I might leave and go to the private school in Chattanooga, or I might go to school in England, where my mother's from."

"The boy with the hair on his face," he said, "is slow on account of he didn't get his air being born, but if he could think to know where England or Tennessee was, he'd wish you happy travels."

When I laughed, a hard shell around him cracked, letting out a sudden brightness, as he said, "You thought about taking snuff or something to take the gleaming glare off your teeth? You always so shiny in the face? I bet you stay clean. I took and saved up for some Ipana, but the man came to the door with a parakeet in a suitcase the other day and asked me what I'd give him for it. Your family use Ipana? Your mama got nice teeth? It was some English that kept house that summer my mama cooked in Atlanta, eight, nine of them, and three, four right teeth in their head if you could of stomached counting. I got to sleep on a feather mattress, though."

Before I could ask for details, his thin, large-eyed mother came outside and stood by him, holding a square of calico, and as she opened it and sorted out a few nickels and pennies, she smiled at me, saying, "I heard it was a new family down the road. You must be the girl. I need to send Ephraim to the store after a snack of supper, if you care to walk with him."

I was clueless as to what grade of supper could be bought for the eighteen cents she warned him not to lose along the way or waste on another trick bird. He stood and brushed dirt off his long legs and combed his fingers through an unruly head of dusty black hair, telling his mother, "Last time, they said they'd let me get some Ipana on time. I wish you'd allow it."

When she said they weren't buying tooth powder on credit, explaining how that kind of lax attitude about finances was what had condemned her to work like an animal since his father died and left them under a burden of debts, I took the time to consider the ridges on his fingernails, how deeply furrowed they were, like the plowed field across the road. And even though everyone our age was snaggle-toothed, his few stray crooks of outsize permanent teeth appeared to be coming in rotten.

Noticing me inspecting, his mother said, "He still looks a little catching, but he's stopped being, so you won't get something on the way to the store. When you get there, I'd appreciate it if you stood behind him and didn't let the man sell him casings and call it sausage, like he did the other day."

"I know how to speak up," Ephraim told her.

"Oh," I said, "I didn't speak up my name. It's Katy, and I'd like to go, but I should be going home now."

I couldn't say my mother was making a pork loin and a chocolate cake for my and my father's first school days, or that she was serving dinner early to allow time to drive to the dime store for fresh notebooks, lead, and all the other merchandise I'd been fantasizing about that would amount to a total of a great deal more than eighteen cents. I didn't know about country people and their food habits and home ways, but I understood from Ephraim's sudden, irritated distraction that he was probably regarding how unnecessarily greedy the clerk had been to rook a woman and a child out of a dime's worth of nourishment and how he should've spoken up against it, or maybe how the casings had slipped around in his mouth.

My father had just finished an advanced degree in secondary education from the University of Georgia and taken on a small, new academy for problem boys, and my mother had been raised on Edgewater Road in London. Her parents had been domestics, but my meaning is she was wholly unfamiliar with the fatalistic outlook of rural people who're extremely clever and efficient at enduring hunger, heat, disease, and poverty but too paralyzed to change anything. That was what I heard when Ephraim's mother told him, "You need to run on by yourself, then, and if you can't get anything but what amounts to nothing, make sure to get a cracker to go with it."

It was going to be an awful errand. I blurted, "If you want to come to my house and let me catch you up on school, you could stay and eat supper."

When his mother asked him if that's what he wanted to do, he said, "No, but I might." She looked at me hard as we were walking away, wondering, I know now, if he was going to return from my ideal environment despising her.

Since our move, my mother had occupied herself with transforming the depression that had begun washing over her in sick waves early in 1925, when my father announced the summer move to north Georgia, which had a reputation for being grindingly impoverished. On the rattling drive down, she'd mournfully narrated the scenery, stark one minute and in chaotic disrepair the next; but in the five or six weeks we'd been living there, her impulsive generosity had sent her into the same falling-down houses she'd criticized with buckets of eggs, sides of ham, bottles of Mercurochrome, and in several cases the county health nurse. Had she come across Ephraim before I did, she would've had him at our table earlier.

She and my father made certain dinner went off normally, and they made Ephraim comfortable. He didn't despise his mother when he returned to his house; he wasn't capable of it. Later, he told me he'd actually felt a little better there, knowing he was continually welcomed to the food and love at mine, and also because we'd come to the agreement that first evening, without having to mention any word pertaining to it, that we were friends, in the deepest order of love—indefinitely, for good, infinitely.

two

STAYING AS FIXED ON ONE ANOTHER AS TWO YOUNG people can be without eloping and setting up isolated housekeeping away from the ordinary run of things, we understood when accommodations needed to be made to grant wishes never spoken and protect large and small bestowals of trust. By the time we married in 1937, like everyone, we'd accumulated our shoals of habits and ways that could've been shifted about or changed outright, but we didn't go for one another with a view to an ideal. In 1997, when complications from a fairly simple heart attack settled in with no apparent intent to resolve themselves, my emotions felt manhandled for some ruthless purpose I was blind to—a world away, you see, from the careful way I'd been treated at home for sixty years, by a mother and father, then a husband.

I expected to recover, as there'd been no reason for decline other than age. But then the custom of order in our home began falling away into a kind of continual misery. The cardiac problems that remained with Ephraim after his fever had been only intermittent, sending him to the hospital only twice, both times in his late seventies. They were always followed by a recovery that'd bring him back around to his routine. No one who knew us predicted I'd be the one to get sick and stay that way. My own disbelief grew into a kind of shattering, ear-ringing sense of unreality that made it seem as though I were standing at a high window, watching another person go around in this waking nightmare.

I began to hear nothing but black news and dismal forecasts from doctors I'd already thanked for their services and said earnest good-byes to; and maybe, I thought, distance is called for and granted when decisions need to be made that a person would prefer to die rather than make. The sense of unreality was a refuge, and though I knew I had to see my way clear of it, I needed time to bear the truth that I would be going away soon, and that the chief advantage of love, the sensation of being separate but one and thoroughly filled in body and spirit but vacant without one another, was going to stay behind and harm my husband.

Worry about him had less to do with keeping him clean and nourished, more to do with company, and of the correct kind. He couldn't listen to chatter, so when I'd picture women rotating in and out of the house from the services I found in the yellow pages, I'd also see him cringing; and when I called a few women who advertised themselves as home-health nurses or something of that nature, seeking employment in the Rome and Atlanta papers, I saw Ephraim locked in the bathroom half the day, too polite to dismiss them.

Though each of us had been an only child, and though we lacked the large extended families that generally come forward to care for a widower themselves or make arrangements for a nursing home, we had a community of friends who'd helped enormously during my two-year decline. But no sooner than I could list the people who'd be willing to step in and more or less take Ephraim in hand, I'd picture him returning from the cemetery and urging them to take their casserole dishes and go. He'd close the door behind them, muttering to explain that he was fine but then telling himself he'd fare better without the embarrassment of their mercy.

Believing he'd feel less lonely if he were alone, he'd go into the new solitude with a degree of false hopefulness. He'd push away regret at having sent our son Wyatt and his wife Ann back to California directly from the cemetery, but then he'd look at the clock to mark the time they'd be getting to their overpriced house in San Francisco and go ahead and accept the oncoming sorrow of knowing they weren't going to call. The next time they called, they'd say they hadn't wanted to disturb him, a foolish lie that had caused us both an infuriating, hot ache around our hearts—an ache that we never learned to thoroughly relieve.

Thinking that their refusal to call on this particular day, when they knew he was alone and grieving, amounted to cruelty, he'd pull the back door open, rattling the windowpanes.

Then he'd take several turns around the backyard before he stopped to see to the pigeons he kept by the edge of our neighbor's farm—the parakeet was gone by the end of grammar school, and he began with the pigeons. Our house was on the last sliver of town property, so standing at the kitchen window, I was able to look to the left toward downtown Rome and see the kind of place I'd been born into, and he could look in the other direction and see a raw clay field and the dark wall of trees.

I could see him go back inside with the goal of getting upstairs without running or screaming, walking harder and faster toward our bedroom to satisfy an urge that could come upon him like a craving, the need to fold his slender, angular self into a small package on my side of the bed and close his eyes. He was aware of his strengths, and so he knew he owned every quality of will a man would need to lie there and not get up until they finally came in to pull a cover over and lift him. Imagining the full scene of him there shocked me in a way that made the coming sensation of my own death seem like a fairly negligible terror.

three

ON THE MORNING I WAS DISCHARGED FROM THE hospital for the last trip home I'd be making, a woman named Rose came into my room, and it was as though a quick, expert hand had slipped in and untangled a tedious knot. Glenda, the lead intensive care nurse, who'd given her permission to come in and see whether I'd consider hiring her to go home with me, let her in the door, saying, "I told her you were waiting for your husband, Mrs. Doyal, but she doesn't need more than a minute. I told her how I've looked after you and Mr. Doyal enough to know being in your home wouldn't be as much of a job of work as it'd be a pleasure, and I also mentioned how you used to be a librarian, you know, over by the high school."

I'd developed a peculiar sympathy for Glenda. When she was close by, moving me from the gurney onto the bed after

I'd waited a few hours or days in the emergency room or pushing sedatives into the line they'd bored into my chest after all the usable veins had been spent, it was difficult to keep from slurring an apology for her having to do the same repetitious, futile work to my body. Glenda had never treated Ephraim or me with anything but good manners—in stark contrast to the vulgar way an emergency room doctor called Dr. Woodward expressed his impatience when I'd been brought in two weeks before, when he saw the multiple admissions in my chart, mumbled my age and diagnosis, and said too loudly from the hall, "Seventy-nine, congestive heart failure, get her the fuck out of my ER." Glenda was a smart, rawboned country girl I could trust to chase anyone or anything that didn't matter from the room while I was dying.

Associating me with a library and all the quietude, good manners, and proper English it implied was a method friends and family had sometimes used to serve notice to potentially loud or foulmouthed strangers. As Glenda spoke, Rose sat by the door and pushed the skin above her knees and then her breasts into a serious-minded white skirt and blouse which argued against the amount of red around her. Her sturdily vigorous figure said she could jump over and crack open my chest, but her hair, cheeks, lipstick, and purse said she'd spent a great deal of time dancing—a contrast of texture that says there's the substance of history in a life.

Before Glenda closed the door, she said, "If it's too much to have on your mind today, Mrs. Doyal, I wish you'd still take Rose's information. You may not realize the kind of help you could use in the house until you get there, with your son and his wife having to leave so soon again and all."

I'd been sitting on the bed, putting unused medical condiments into my satchel—alcohol swabs, packets of antibiotic ointment—and although Glenda wasn't going to turn me in and cause me to be billed, I stopped and pulled a pillow over the things, not to look tacky or like the elderly, desperately thrifty lunatic who'd been discharged from the room the day before, going on and on about how much wear she could get out of a pair of paper slippers and how good the blue gripper socks were for opening jars and grabbing the stair rails to her basement, where she slept because of the free cool.

I said, "Thank you both, but I'll have my husband, and he's been enough help after these stays."

"But your husband," Glenda said, "looked like a patient himself when I saw him here yesterday evening. When he shows up to get you, I'm taking his blood pressure, and if I don't like it, I'm calling his cardiologist, and then I'm calling yours so he can be the one to say you're not getting out of here until you have some help."

"If we bought those life alert deals," I said, "or those things where you clap and the fire department comes and hacks the door down, would that satisfy you? Something has to, if I'm not going to be trapped here if Ephraim fails his physical."

Rose held one hand up off the enormous red purse in her lap, and when I indicated she was more or less called on, she twisted around to Glenda and then looked at me, saying,

"Not meaning to correct, but it's the light you clap to turn on, and it's a sorry product, good for nothing but driving you out of your mind. I worked at Sears Roebuck in the home department and liked to of went insane with a dozen of them going on and off continuously."

Glenda said, "I've got to run, but Rose, remember Mrs. Doyal's been in the hospital a couple of weeks and, you know, she's probably a fan of having things a little more hushed than most."

I wanted to hear whatever she had to say, and when I asked her to continue, she said, "You know how it goes when you can't tolerate. I'm not many things, and I've never been one of those."

I remembered how Ephraim's mother would make the same open-ended declaration about herself and asked, "One of those what?"

"Tolerate the wrong things," she said. "It was my last job in the retail industry, though I got a high reference—you can check on a paper I intend to leave with you. And the other, the thing you wear around your neck, it turns into a crying-wolf situation from the point of view of the individuals that rescue you on account of it's set on a hair trigger, and if you breathe hard on it or bump it, all hell will break loose, and, yes, they will blow in your house like it's a mass murder going on, and if you're not in severe shape, what I mean to say is, if they get enough false alarms, when the real one comes, they're likely to rear back and say to hell with you."

Already convinced of it, I asked, to be certain, "You like bleach a great deal, don't you?"

"Yes ma'am," she said, "but not spray starch."

When she shook her head to prove how violently she disliked what she called "cheating starch, and a half-assed way of managing," I saw the clustered fruit earrings her hair had been hiding, and I regretted every time I'd seen them on the markdown rack in a department store and told myself only hard or loose women would wear them. I'd question the character of someone who'd broadcast such a cheap commentary on herself and go away feeling superior and handsome, and by the next time I looked in a mirror, I'd see old, thick, worn—and then, confused, I'd have to wait to find Ephraim and the reflection of myself in his eyes.

Whether she'd worn the fruit or pearls, she believed there was honor in domestic hustle, smiling to describe how much of a relic she was, with what sounded like an adoration of Argo starch and blue plastic-wrapped refrigerated shirts, the grout-whitening paste she'd been tempted to patent, how she could compromise garden-up cooking only as far as Minute Rice. Of all the things about her available to tell the story I needed to hear, whether in her rush of words or her solidly rigorous composure, it was the particular ridged furrows of her fingernails, which I could see from the bed, that said my husband would feel safe with her from the beginning and contented with her eventually. They were in the same condition as his. He wouldn't have to see hands cleaning, ironing, sewing, and resting in her lap and have the difference remind him of mine—the hands of the individual you live with for sixty years or more, you see, being an irrevocable vision.

He didn't need rude, jolting reminders; he needed memories that were there, of Sunday mornings after Wyatt moved away to school and we were finally without the responsibility of exposing a child to religion. In bed one of those mornings, he took my hands and turned them in and out of the light, touching over the surface of my nails, saying, "I stay evermore grateful to your daddy for being sober, working to feed you so well, keep you so well-cared for. I wish I'd shown him these hands to let him know how I kept you."

"He knew," I said. "He never questioned it."

He said, "I know, Katy, but still, it'd be something to say, how you've stayed well-cared for, smooth nails, smooth as nails. Katy kept very, very well."

four

I F ROSE HADN'T APPEARED, I WOULD'VE HAD TO GO home that morning and wait to get sick enough to be picked up off the floor and brought back, unable to rest evenings in bed beside Ephraim because of the hard regret of having so few left and the extremes that began to seem realistic and inevitable. Before I talked with Rose, I felt like my face was being pushed down onto a picture everyone knew revolted me and didn't care, pressing me closer, hectoring me so that my eyes stayed open and didn't miss anything of the view.

I had to see him ignoring help knocking, and so it goes on and on, but he doesn't shift from his place, and after a time he realizes he's capable of shutting himself off from his loathing of crawling things and could give a damn about how vulnerable to the workings of biology he's leaving himself. He could be almost senselessly stubborn by nature, and in dealing with our son sometimes, he was capable of fixing himself to a position he knew to be utterly wrong or illogical and taking it to incredible limits, but it would be something else entirely if he decided he didn't care who discovered him. If he said aloud, "I could care less," in the same tone he used every time Wyatt told Ephraim that the way he dressed, talked, and carried himself when we visited him at Vanderbilt was unbearable, he'd toss aside the worst horrors and continue to lie there and starve himself.

A stranger with malnourished hands held better promise for Ephraim's future than our son and his wife did. They'd always been blunt about being less likely to leave California than Ephraim and I were to live anyplace other than Georgia. After he retired from his position as a civil engineer with the railroad and the investment bonanza made it ridiculous for me not to take an early retirement to enjoy being home with him, they seemed staggered whenever he and I traveled somewhere that required crossing the Mississippi River. It wasn't that they considered us frail; they'd just never credited us with enough creativity to invent an itinerary or the nerve to go anywhere English wasn't spoken.

Although either one of them would've blistered Dr. Woodward for his rude remarks, they were also inclined to reduce us to infancy—as if we hadn't lived at all; hadn't endured a Depression and a world war; hadn't been rich, poor, and in between, as though our time alive had less value than theirs. They placed an unwarranted emphasis on being proficient at operating a computer; and when the library, by coincidence, converted from the card catalog system to a network, blathering one evening, I happened to mention the change to Wyatt, who told me that was why I'd quit and forgave my fear of admitting it. They saw Ephraim's idiocy as thorough and potentially dangerous. The week before I met Rose, when the three of them met over my bed in intensive care, they assumed I was sufficiently knocked out and wouldn't hear the fate Wyatt and Ann intended to introduce Ephraim to as soon as it became necessary.

Much like now, I was highly aware but unable to shout, for instance, and tell my son to stop playing such a flip and ridiculous game with his father's emotions and admit what benefit he had in mind for himself should his father lose his reason and commit to their scheme.

Holding my hand, he said, "Dad, Ann and I discussed it, you know, the last time Mom was this sick, and we decided what we should do is sell the house in California and get something in Florida and have you move in with us there. We can look for a condominium with a ground-floor bedroom, something on the beach. I know you may not believe it, Dad, but I'm willing, and you know it's for your own good, you know, the climate."

"And heat to death," Ephraim said, "the year-round with the urine-smelling old sonofabitches baking? You're stupider than I thought you were if you've spent more than the duration of an hour-long drunk considering it."

Ann's parents had moved from Massachusetts to Miami. She said, "It's amazed me, Mr. Doyal. My father's eighty-two and looks seventy, same with my mother. They've had ten very nice years there."

"Amazed me, too," Ephraim said, "the other Christmas at your house, when your father took a drink and told me he felt like he'd been bound, gagged, and shoved in the trunk so he could be taken to Miami Beach and forced to live piddling around a concrete-block village because his wife was tired of looking fat in winter clothes. He told me not to tell anybody, but under the circumstances, I think he'd want me to."

"This isn't funny," Wyatt said. "Sooner rather than later there're going to be some issues to resolve about your care."

Ephraim said, "Do I look that elderly to you? Do I smell it?"

"Certainly not," Ann said, "but we were thinking, since my parents were thriving in Florida, and Wyatt and I are finally at a stable enough place to feel like we could make a few changes, we honestly thought a move would work for all of us."

"For one," Ephraim said, "it makes no sense to say you finally have your feet on the ground, so it's time to create a major disruption. But I'm old and lacking a psychology practice, so you can ignore it, but don't ignore me when I tell you Florida is the one place Katy and I wouldn't travel to—hell, couldn't travel to—because we neither one believed it was going to be real when we got there."

More or less together, they said, "But you went to Las Vegas every Thanksgiving."

"And we knew it wasn't real before we got there," Ephraim said. "Or it could've been another kind of real, going on alongside this, and we thoroughly enjoyed doing any god-damn thing you wanted to do, any time of the day or evening. Your mother sat at a slot machine so long one time she liked to of had to wear her arm in a sling. We tell you that or decide it was nobody's business?"

Wyatt said, "You told us."

"Then we're straight on the fact that I'll do what I want to do," Ephraim said, "and I could care less why you think I should be required to behave otherwise."

"Because," Wyatt said, "I already know how determined you're going to be not to properly look after yourself. You've already started, the last couple of years, using Mom's heart disease as an excuse not to manage your own sorry health."

Ephraim said, "What would make you think I'd leave my life to go live in a concrete village with you and some damp strangers to be treated with this kind of disrespect?"

"You can't look after the house, Mr. Doyal, not realistically," Ann said.

Ephraim said, "They have places that advertise help, but that'd fall under my business. What about yours, though? Is it that many in a retirement state that call for switching their makeups?"

Ann counseled people through the change of their sex, and after she told Ephraim he was right, that she wouldn't expect the same volume of traffic if she opened an office in Florida, she said, "But I wasn't planning to work there, you see, because I was thinking we'd finally get pregnant."

"I'm going to ignore the 'we,'" Ephraim said, "but tell me

why you've continually put it off until Katy's like this. Did you not hear her doctor say she can't stand another bout with the fluid? Did you not hear that, and did you not hear all the times over the past ten years Katy asked you about having a baby?"

Wyatt said, "It didn't, doesn't, concern her or anyone, Dad. It's been our decision to wait, and I thought you'd appreciate this, until everything had come together."

"And who paid most of the bill," Ephraim asked, "for it all coming together? If your mother recovers this time, you'd better keep the family plan to yourself, or hide and watch the cruelty kill her. Do you know she went without a new car she needed, back before we had any order of money, so we could furnish you the down payment you wanted for the first large house you didn't need? You'll answer it was just money, but it was our labor and time going out to the other side of the country with nothing but having it taken for granted coming back toward us. Looking at her now, knowing what's coming, there was so much other we could've been doing with the peace of mind we shot on worry. You'd have me believe your life doesn't concern her, if you could, but you can't."

Ann began crying, apologizing, telling Wyatt they should leave his father alone with me for a while, and after a time, Wyatt said, "It's severe, Dad. It starts feeling severe when I don't understand what you want me to do."

"Same as she told you all your life," Ephraim said, "be kind and do your best."

Wyatt said, "Right now, I meant."

"You can let your mother rest," Ephraim told him, "and go out of this room knowing you owe her more."

In a week and a half, Wyatt and Ann went home, as Ephraim often said, "to live squarely within our means." He spent most of his days at the hospital and several nights asleep in the vinyl lay-back chair with his head propped on the windowsill. Glenda offered him empty beds, but he'd say he was comfortable. I had to explain to her that he actually was. Sleep was all the same to him; he didn't measure its quality. He once slept for six hours on a bench on the deck of a boat, sailing in the rain from Normandy to Marseille.

He'd stayed at home the night before I was discharged, knowing how upsetting it'd be for me to walk into a scrambled house. He said, "It's never happened for you to come home to a mess, but let me go sweep and wash a dish or two regardless, and I'll see you as soon as the doctor says I can have you tomorrow."

"You'll neither sweep nor wash a dish," I told him. "What's been undone since Ann left the house, the neighborhood fell on and cleaned."

I hadn't told him I'd heard her and Wyatt's plan to start a family now, had no intention to, and there was no reason for it other than to stir up misery. It was on my mind when Glenda let Rose and her blunt glory in the room, how few rights parents are justified to claim in a married child's life, how little permission sacrifice had bought.

five

THINK I MAY'VE SAID ALOUD, "I DON'T KNOW WHAT HIS father and I expected," just before Rose came in. After she and I'd talked awhile and my satchel was ready, she wouldn't let me carry it to the door. I wanted to be able to wait on the bed with nothing in my hands to prevent me from getting up and out the door with Ephraim the instant he arrived for me.

"Rose," I said, "you can tell I'm ready to be out of here, and I wish I could tell you I'm just as eager to have someone, particularly you, doing for me once I get home. Does it make sense or seem in any way reasonable that I don't want what time my husband and I have left to be watered down?"

"Time he spends talking to somebody else in the house," she said, "he could be spending with you. I can back you on that, Mrs. Doyal, same way I can you taking home hospital supplies they're going to dun you halfway to a heart attack for anyway. Some people wouldn't see things that way, but I happen to be one of these that do. You and he need rich time, and if I were you, I'd take it, but if you need me farther on down, I want you to call my house or send Glenda to the bank I clean or the Pepsi plant to find me, either one."

"You work how many jobs?" I asked her.

"Two and a half," she said, "to three. No set schedule except at the bottling place, though. The rest of the time, I tend to keep rubber hours so I can expand out into office cleaning or nursing for people Glenda shows me around to."

"Do you get tired?" I asked.

"Yes" she said, "but I sleep."

I said, "As long as I'm asking questions, Rose, do you mind saying how old you are?"

"Not at all," she said, "I'm fifty-three, so I remember when you could get something at the drugstore strong enough to control your hair and a headache."

I sat on the foot of the bed, looking out the window, and thinking I saw Ephraim six floors below, I said, "You can't find either now, but Rose, I need you to tell me one more thing, and quickly, if you can. What I need is, I want you to tell me what kind of person you believe you are."

"Well," she said, "you know I love to work and take care of individuals and their objects, houses, clothes, and so forth. Glenda can tell you I'm not on the hunt for well-off sick people to sponsor me."

"I know," I told her. "It's evident. What I'm saying, Rose,

is tell me why I'd be able to rest if you were in my home, you see, alone with my husband, if I had to be somewhere else."

She said, "I can't say because I'm not married. I like to've been married once, but I can list out shoals of wives who'd tell you I can bathe a husband without laying the wrong kind of hand on him."

"Not safe from you, Rose, safe with you," I told her.

"Oh," she said, "if I was in charge of him, he'd know he was being cared for."

I said, "So if you were to step in as I stepped out, he wouldn't have to feel like he was falling."

"No," she said, "not at all, Mrs. Doyal."

"Katy."

"Yes, Katy, then what you're needing to know is if Glenda appears over by the bottling plant one morning and asks if I remember the lady she took me to at the hospital, the calm one that looked weak in the face—if she says they've just had to take you from your home and she believes it'd be right for me to go over there—you want me to go."

"Yes, Rose," I told her, "I think so."

"But you need to understand," she said, "he's going to be falling when I get there."

"I don't want him to. That's what I need you to keep from happening," I said.

She said, "I wish I could, but nobody can. The best I can do is pick him up and work to keep him that way."

"And you wouldn't allow him to linger," I said, "while you went, I don't know, dancing."

"Oh, I'll dance," she said, "but I don't go but as far as the kitchen to do it. I keep a radio running in the window."

I said, "But the red, you know, and your figure."

"This is my mother's body," she said, "and her mother's. I was born into it, and color keeps me from being bored getting from one end of the day to the other alone, like a kind of hobby I can carry—you know, portable. The ways I've figured out to organize my life and hold my body while I'm going and going at it, I like color, Katy."

"But," I said, "I don't hear anything about a man. Ephraim and I've been together since we were eight years old, Rose, seventy-three years. How'd you accomplish feeling as settled in yourself alone?"

She said, "By not dwelling on it, probably, but also, very early, when I was very young, it felt the future was going to be exactly as it's been."

"What kind of man was your father?" I asked her, knowing.

"You already know, Katy," she said. "The few I tried to run around with all turned out to favor him. I wasn't willing to borrow damage."

"But children?"

"I've helped raise a dozen," she said, "who come around to care about how I'm doing better than my own probably would."

"Tell it," I said. "You'll meet my son and his wife directly. He's the kind that feels cheated every few minutes of the day, but I know he can be more contented eventually, and his wife, I'm sorry to say I don't know her well enough to explain her basic nature. I believe they're planning to have a baby, you know, just in time."

"For you," she said, "not to sew for."

"But you can."

"Yes," she said, "and will, but you knew that, and you knew your husband would have no choice but to fall."

"I did," I told her. "But tell me again, you can pick him up and keep him standing. You can't let him lie there."

"Look at my hands," she said, "as hard as you did when I got here."

"I have," I said.

Looking at her watch, she said, "But Katy, your husband, wasn't he on his way to take you home?"

I said, "Glenda must've grabbed him on his way to the room, to see, you know, whether he still looked like a patient."

"Then," she said, "why don't I see what's happening?"

"Thank you," I told her, "but it's not time."

When she said I was right and handed me her page of references, saying she needed to go home and get ready for her shift, I followed her to the door to say, "If you help me, Rose, you wouldn't have to report to work on another bottling line."

"The good thing," she said, "is it doesn't involve talking to customers who could be rude. I could do any job of work but clerking."

I said, "But, Rose, what I'm trying to say is if you took over at my house for me, you could leave the other."

"One job?" she asked.

"Yes," I said, "do you think you could manage?"

"To be one of those?" she asked.

"Who can sleep of an evening?" I said.

"Shamed to say it," she said, "but, yes, and shamed to ask, but I was wondering whether you lived in a brick or wood house."

When I said it was brick, she smiled and said, "I know it's nice, but Katy, if it's something like the oven temperature a certain degree off or a leak behind a something, I hope you'll try to leave me a note. I'd feel better, wouldn't you?"

"Yes," I said, "and I admit I was planning to write out what they'll run in the paper to keep somebody else from doing it, but it's crazy-making when I think too long about it, and I'd hate for people to think I was intending to control. Does that make sense?"

Taking my hands, she said, "It does, and the people that know you are already going to know what you could say about yourself, and the strangers that turn to that section of the paper to read about strangers aren't worth the time or the paper, but what is, at least to me, is knowing what to do if your bobbin tends to drop or whether the doors tend to swell in the summer, or what your husband prefers to eat and whether he feels better having a new tube of toothpaste waiting for him when he runs out of the present one—I'd be grateful to know whatever comes to mind that matters, whatever you want to leave said."

six

KATHERINE KELLER DOYAL

"Katy"

Born December 30, 1918, in Athens, Georgia. Longtime resident of Rome. Daughter of the late Elliot Banks Keller and Eugenia Davis Keller. Wife of Ephraim Lowe Doyal. Mother of Wyatt Lowe, who resides in Petaluma, California, with his wife, Ann. Beloved member of the community and retired librarian at Rome High School, she traveled frequently and was well-known for her love of hearth and home. Passed from this life on December 28, 1998. Graveside services and interment at Grace Memorial Park; the family will receive visitors immediately following at home, 4820 Brattlewood Road. The family requests that contributions to the Atlanta area MotherRead be made in lieu of flowers.

~

THE YOUNG WOMAN FROM THE FUNERAL HOME WHO was assigned to write my obituary had only some disjointed answers to the few questions Ephraim could sit still for, and though it was difficult at first, the writing moved along quickly once she decided which category of small-town elderly white female I belonged to and that she could stay entirely on the surface because that's all there was to people like me. I'd never had patience with the timid women she made me over into, and I'd always felt judged by them. Nobody who read it would credit what this numbed version of me is doing now—hovering about in a state of something like perpetual titillation, waiting to be with her husband, waiting for his death and his resurrection, his new life with her in their new home on the other side of air.

In one of the theories of what becomes of us, people continue to be what they were, whether it was sad, mean-willed, empathetic, self-absorbed, easygoing, curious; and in my case at least, that feels to be true, as my most constant sensation is a familiar love. I was and am the love I had with my husband, and so it is little wonder that when eternity presented itself to me, I felt returned all the way into the one moment embedded down into the night we were married, when I first reached up my arms and pulled his body inside mine. Time has become that one adored instant, spiritually outstanding.

Ephraim had always been in extraordinary spiritual condition, probably because he was agile at shifting the weight of his concerns and directing himself through mazes that confuse people who can't or won't decide what is and isn't important to them. Maybe owing to an inherited portion of his mother's fatalism, he was less adamant about his physical health, doing nothing more or less than what he was told to manage the heart problems that had begun in 1925 with his summer fever.

He ignored opportunities to fight for his health; new ideas and advancements didn't faze him. If the doctor finished an examination and did anything to indicate he was on the verge of describing a procedure he'd just learned about, Ephraim would keep buttoning his shirt, and without looking up, he'd say, "I'm sorry, Russell, but I told you twenty years ago I didn't feel like it."

After the second attack, when he wouldn't hear the suggestion that a valve replacement would prevent another problem in the same area, Russell, who was also our down-the-street neighbor said, "But what about Katy and what she wants for you, Ephraim, for herself? I cannot understand why you wouldn't consent to anything that could give you more mornings to be out in the flower beds together, the way I saw you when I passed by on the way to work this morning."

Russell looked at me to argue, but I had to tell him, "What I have to say about Ephraim's health doesn't matter."

"It doesn't," Ephraim said, "because either one of us could fall out in a pile of peat moss tomorrow, and if we stayed there and got preserved in it, like the miniature man we saw at the museum, it's as close as we'll get to being around forever."

"So you're fine," I told him on the way home, "for your last thought to be, 'If I'd had a random outpatient procedure, I might not be about to widow my wife.' That seems fair and rational to you?"

"What's rational," he said, "is that a seventy-eight-year-old man is likely to die in ten, twelve years, regardless of how many mangling improvements he's had made on his heart and no matter whether his main diet habit was lard or lettuce. I'm not willing for the time to be urgent. I'd prefer to spend it the way we would've fifty years ago, before they were continually rushing you with updates on the information they gave you last week. I don't want to be crammed and pushed at the end, Katy. I don't want to feel jerked out of here. It's the last thing you have. Not to say I expect to enjoy it, but you'd think they'd look at a man, a veteran, for God's sake, and leave him alone about how he believes he'd be the most comfortable when the time's come for him to, well, leave alone."

seven

M Y DYING WAS ACCOMPLISHED WITH BEAUTIFUL ease, no more extraordinary than the act of walking from one room into another. It happened quietly, at 5:45 on a frozen, gray-dark morning, two days before my eightieth birthday. I'd been in the kind of slow, vague failure that exhausts a body into accepting the last blow against it with a form of resignation that's unbearably too much like gratitude. I'd been decidedly terminal since a stroke on the morning of Christmas eve, when I fell in the kitchen after a vessel gave way and allowed a warm outpouring of blood into my brain, just after I'd put Rose's letter in a drawer and closed it.

Ephraim was on his way through the house to find me and ask why I hadn't been able to rest and what I'd been doing since I got up at three. I'd intended to tell him about a terrible dream, nearly a nightmare, that featured the insane, treacher-

ous man in *Kind Hearts and Coronets* and see what he could say
to keep the unease from lingering into the day and the evening
we were going to spend in bed at the Ritz-Carlton in Atlanta,
a place we used to run away to and often said would be a wonderful place to die in.

It may take a lifetime to reach the instant, but there'll come
a time when you realize that nothing can be helped and you've
already accepted it. Mine arrived as one system after the other
began shutting down, resigning from my body more quickly
than things would've proceeded if my heart had been strong
enough to save just itself from drowning. Soon, it felt as
though a lone and exhausted bit of nerve in one very unalert
corner of my head was carrying the load for what remained
but couldn't manage another whit of effort, and then I heard
what sounded deep inside my ears like a quiet sigh that carried
power away from a few odd, out-of-the-way places. Any last
quick that had stayed dormant through the winter, buried
underneath the wasting, began to stir and arrange itself to rise
out of me, through the tip ends of my fingers, lazily willing,
like a familiar patron who dozes off and is kindly nudged to
leave a theater when the movie's over.

But lights were not coming up; they were leaving, slowly,
and though I saw nothing, I was certain that my mother was
in the room with me, over by the door, turning down my
lamp, asking the others to be quiet so her daughter could rest.
There was wonder and relief inside the blackness and silence,
no movement except something like a shrinking back into
what I had imagined an atom to be, a sort of retreat into

nothing and everything, an unexpected and wonderful accomplishment of perfection—there was the purity of affection and understanding, all wrapped around, as I've described, with my husband's love. Anyone would be justified to ask whether the sensation wasn't the love of God I was reawakening into, but I'd never been certain whether I'd truly believed in Him or only let people assume I did because of the instant uproar that would've followed the slightest expression of doubt.

The source of the love didn't call to be analyzed as it spread out into the space where fear and pain had been, and there wasn't a need to stay watchful for what was due to happen next. What could happen was already taking place in every second of every minute or had taken place in this mixed lot of events, no matter if they'd occurred in Ephraim's life or my son's or in whatever name this new experience of time could be called.

A view sharpened of Ephraim sitting down in a blue chair in the hall to wait for Glenda to come out and bring him to me. He put his head in his hands, hiding his face like a child who's done something wrong and wants it all to be gone the next time he looks up; but as long as he was looking, he checked to be sure he'd worn matching shoes and zipped his trousers, not thinking, clueless as to where he'd left the car. Having his head lowered, he hoped, would commit warm blood to flow to parched places and allow him to stand up and speak sensibly when he needed to answer questions or ask about what was scheduled to happen to me. Faint and dry-mouthed since Glenda called to say things were over, he hadn't called Wyatt because he didn't want to hear his son admit, deny, or ignore the fact that he'd been a sonofabitch and a conscienceless taker.

If there is a switch that makes one's capacity for empathy into an active, motivating force, I still had no way to be sure whether mine had been disabled or if it had gone missing. There was only a benign grade of concern for the weight of misery pulling inside his chest and no guilt for having been released from the worry and responsibility for curing it. The year before, I happened to read a novel about a dying woman whose concern for her husband's ability to feed himself when she's gone leads her to freeze a large quantity of prepared food; and knowing the memories Ephraim had to draw from and trusting Rose to do whatever was necessary to care for him was much like watching him open a full freezer, in which everything I was able to give him was at hand. The possibility that Rose wouldn't appear to act on my behalf wasn't nervous-making, as everything about the scene was furnished for her to walk into.

Glenda spoke my mind when she leaned down over me with a lipstick from her pocket, saying, "Here, good, this looks nice on you. I'm going to go out there and get your husband for you, and I'm going to call Rose for him. Don't worry, she'll be here. I'll call your son also, and the doctor for him to come sign these things. Such a long night, and you finally become his business. They work at not being beside people as they're leaving."

Ephraim had closed his eyes, but when he heard someone

coming toward him, scrubbing along without lifting their feet—a habit that irritated us—he looked up to see if the person looked alert enough to follow a small direction. He had a habit of memorizing faces; but thin, long-haired blond young women ran together for him, so he didn't remember that she was the pharmacist he'd accused of trying to poison him during a particularly long span of confusion after anesthesia. She'd taken it personally, and so the episode was reported along with several other of the mindless, vehement ramblings that made him appear to have Alzheimer's disease. She remembered it well and often recounted it as an attack, a kind of false importance she always pushed forward with when she was around intimidating women like Glenda— wishing she could keep her mouth shut, but not able to; actually rehearsing some intelligent, needless remark to have ready should Glenda be at the station. She was jumpy already when she felt something swat across the hem of her skirt, and before she looked to see what it was, she glanced around to see if Glenda was looking to judge her.

She knew she needed to ask what she could do, but she neither wanted to do it herself nor find Glenda. She smiled as though the first and now the second and third swats were tics, but Ephraim said, "Isn't funny, now listen. Please, I need you to go see when I can go see my wife. Nurse, she's in there, forgot I'm waiting."

She smiled and took a maddening amount of time and his energy to say she was sure he'd be called when it was time. He interrupted her, mumbling, "Hate to tell you, but, no, they won't. It's lazy not to go see. Tell Glenda I need to know how much longer. You could've been there and back." She wasn't going to interfere and risk being talked down to, and deciding he was too old and tired to get up and go across the hall himself, she wished him well and left.

Decrepitude wasn't keeping him in his chair—he could've shot across the hall with such force that onlookers would've wondered if a spring had propelled him—but he couldn't open the door on me until he was certain Glenda had removed the breathing tube and IV lines, covered bruises, kneaded the tops of my hands to ease some of the tight swelling from the infiltrated morphine, done whatever else she could to honor his unspoken need that I look like myself.

He was still shaped exactly as he'd been when I met him by the mud hole and had roughly the same weight of hair, only silver now. He'd grown up but not out, so there was little meat around the knees to wedge his elbows into when he leaned forward and put his head in his hands again. A little surprised that he could fall asleep and anxious that Glenda would come out of my room, see him that way, and leave him, he wanted to stay alert. His mind, though, was overly heavy inside his head, and he was immediately drawn so deeply under that when his elbows slipped and his body easily folded over forward, there was no consciousness of care to make him realize he was doing anything unusual by pulling his bony knees toward his chest and going back to sleep on the floor.

To say no instinct took over and forced me to ache at the sight of my husband sounds as cold and hard as his floor. But not only did I feel lifted up out of old concerns by the vague sense of universal goodwill; I'd also organized Rose, who Glenda more or less stepped over his sleeping body to call. As he'd feared, she'd seen him there and decided to let him rest, regardless of the floor, lifting his eyelids and checking his pulse before she walked behind the station and defended her decision to the three nurses who'd been too intently grouped around a bridal magazine to notice he'd fallen.

Taking her phone list out of her desk drawer, she listened to questions about the propriety of letting him stay there, saying, "Deciding if somebody should dye a pair of shoes or buy new ones for a wedding that's a year and a half away isn't my business, but what happens on this floor is, and what's happening right now is Mr. Doyal is free to sleep on it until I've made these calls. If it won't postpone the wedding, I'd appreciate one of you calling the ER for whoever they have on neurology, and if it's the sonofabitch Dr. Woodward they're going to be sending up here, let me know when so I can be elsewhere. If it didn't have to be a neurologist, I swear I'd use a podiatrist. I hate the thought of that man around Mrs. Doyal. She saw enough of him alive."

She was known to make elaborate plans to avoid the ill-mannered ER doctor. As she was calling Wyatt, it occurred to Glenda that they both used arrogance to hide similar insecurities around women. Believing Wyatt's first impulse would be to demand a confession of everything she'd been too ignorant to do for me, she was relieved when he didn't answer. While she was leaving a message to call the hospital as soon as he could, he was watching her number glow in the dark by his bed, not able to lift his arm to reach it, suddenly weighted down by a smothering burden of black air that had been hanging over the bed for the two days he'd been lying in it with his clothes and tennis shoes on, rolling around on top of plates and cups, empty popcorn bags, and beer bottles.

Ann had been across town, taking advantage of a three-night special at the Fairmont Hotel, the birthday present she'd given herself after she correctly predicted that Wyatt would get her an anonymous-feeling gift and hand it to her unwrapped, saying he hadn't tried harder because she was so difficult to please. As she packed for the hotel, he argued against the connection she'd just claimed existed between his ability to show love and her desire to try to prolong the marriage with either the move or the baby they'd stupidly told his father about prematurely, before Ephraim could realize he was miserable alone and become naturally more receptive.

She also reminded Wyatt of her parents' warning that she wouldn't inherit a dime if she allowed them to decline and die without their favorite daughter near them in Florida. He had a habit of hanging his head like his father when he felt scolded, and she told him he could at least look at her while she was on her way out, saying, "I saw a thoughtless birthday present coming, Wyatt, and now I'm seeing me in Florida with my parents and you shut up alone in that little house with your father, no wife, no baby, and nothing to take the edge off the misery. Think about that while I'm at the hotel, enjoying a private birthday present. And as for not being able to satisfy me with a birthday present, Wyatt, that's bullshit."

"No, it's not," he said. "It's not bullshit, Ann."

"Yes," she said, "it is. I would've been thrilled with a box of toothpicks if it came with some indication you love me. You can bet your father never treated your mother like you do me, Wyatt—you know, that's a connection. He's never been ashamed to show he loves her. She's the first thing he thinks of in the morning and the last thing he's aware of in the evening. How you could've been raised with that kind of adoration going on right in front of you and be the way you are is beyond me, and I have a goddamn degree in—well, in human beings."

Scared now and not able to keep himself from showing it, he asked, "How long do you plan to be gone, Ann? Let me get dressed and go with you."

"I'm fine alone," she said. "I'll see you in three days, and I know it's too much to ask, but I can't tell you what it'd mean to me if you could use part of the time to think—no, feel— or you'll be forced to be alone for the rest of your life or else settle for third-rate."

"You're not second-rate," he said. "I don't know what you mean."

"I mean," she said, "a long time ago you said that since you couldn't marry your mother, the second-best woman was me. Well, knowing your mother, being behind her is a pretty goddamn excellent place to be. But I'm thirty-six years old, Wyatt.

I'm too old to beg for affection. I'm too old to consider moving to the other side of the country with a man who won't even hold my hand on the way there."

Finally looking at her, Wyatt said, "I know, Ann, but it's like with my father. I don't know what you want me to do."

She said, "I suggest you think of what he would do if he ever lost his mind and found himself in this situation with his wife. And then I'd do it, Wyatt, sooner rather than later. I mean, after all, you're willing to let your mother die without even letting her know you loved her so much that you wanted to be with a woman who reminded you of her."

"I'm not feeling well right now, Ann," he said, "and suppose something happens to Mom? I mean, her nurse said we shouldn't stay too far from the phone."

"If they call about your mother," she said, "then call me."

He said, "This is getting depressing."

"You should be depressed. I'd be depressed if I were you," she said. "Still, I'm amazed to hear you say it. However, I'm not someone who dislikes myself so thoroughly that I can't aim higher. I want more. As close to death as your mother's been, Wyatt, I wish I could trade places with her long enough for your father to look at me the way he looks at her. Remember his eyes the last time we saw him? They had everything in them. You call me difficult to please, but how hard would it be to give the gift of looking at me in such a loving way?"

eight

ROSE WAS DRESSED FOR THE DAY AND DRINKING coffee on her sofa, paying her bills and watching *The Ladykillers* on the old movie channel, amazed at Alec Guinness's teeth and grateful to Ted Turner for the policy of no commercial interruption that she called the difference between rest and ruination. Glenda expected to call in the middle of her doing as much, and she apologized for interfering before she said, "Rose, you remember Mrs. Doyal, Katy Doyal, the woman I said I'd call you about if something happened to her, remember, because of her husband's condition?"

"Yes," Rose said, taking her cup to the kitchen, cutting off the television set on the way. "She and I talked a great deal that day about me working taking care of him."

Glenda said, "Good. Then could you come on to the hospital? He's here. He went to sleep on the floor while he was waiting to go to her room and, you know, spend some time with her, and if I could make sure you can come ahead on, I'll go ahead and wake him up."

Rose said, "Hold the fort a minute, Glenda. I'm confused. Did she die or is she just worse?"

Glenda said, "She died this morning, Rose, but I'm concerned about Mr. Doyal because, well, I don't know how to put it. I'm worried because he's the way he is. I've been with them both together, by themselves, one sick, the other well, and the other way around, and Mr. Doyal's, well . . ."

"If you were going to say he's the way he is," Rose said, "I wish you'd be more specific. His wife also spoke of him that way, and it'd help to have more to go on, like an adjective, before I meet him."

Glenda said, "The most I think I can say is he's special."

"Which could mean," Rose said, "you're behind his right to keep his retardation private. I can appreciate it, but his wife didn't give me an idea of it. Did he have a brain tumor removed or something?"

"No," Glenda said. "I should've been clearer, but I'm a little addled with him on the floor and not knowing how he's going to manage seeing his wife dead, and then I don't think he's capable of going home. I've left his son a message, but he and his wife have to travel from California, so if you could come and, I don't know, help him get started with everything he'll need to do. If it doesn't occur to him to pay you, I'll take care of it. I have no idea whether he'd consent to hire you permanently, but I believe he'd be interested in some kind of arrangement when he sees the amount of pressure you could take off him."

Rose hadn't told anyone about her commitment to me, and not caring to be quizzed on whether this was the work of the sixth sense, she didn't tell Glenda our arrangement was anything beyond the loose, speculative one she'd described. "I'm able to leave the house in a few minutes," she said, "so if he doesn't wake up between now and then, just leave him for me to take to his wife."

"That could be rough," Glenda said. "I know he's a stranger, but I do this so much up here, Rose, with people old as they usually are when they get here and so sick, and telling someone who's been with another person for fifty years that now they're welcome to stay with the person, the body, for ten minutes or more if they want to, it's a strange permission to be giving."

"All you do is behave like you've had a lobotomy," Rose told her. "Watch for me to be there directly."

I understood Rose's method for getting through anxiety-making situations and had sometimes said I was going to approach a particular ordeal like my Aunt Ruth, who my mother brought back from England in 1929 to stay with us because she'd been given a lobotomy a few years before and was being ignored and left by herself, my mother said, to sit and blow on a low stoop continually. The surgery had been intended to spare her a life of bone-wrenching epileptic seizures, but her family was taking advantage of her disconnection from the world not to trouble themselves to involve her in theirs, something my mother tried to remedy by always including her in whatever we were doing. After she'd been with us a few months, a cat Ephraim caught and somehow domesticated for me ran away and stayed gone. I was so distraught I couldn't speak without weeping, and then one afternoon, my mother, Aunt Ruth, and I were shelling peas at the table, and my aunt said in her flat, blank tone, "I saw the cat fall in the cistern. He's dead, drowned if the fall didn't break his neck."

With my mother and I still sitting there, stunned to be watching, my aunt got up and walked off our property, wandering all afternoon, from later reports of everyone who saw her, through fields and abandoned houses until she found a new cat, which she brought home, squeezed underneath her arm and calling Wyatt, after Ephraim's favorite cowboy figure. Many years later, we named our son this to remind us of Aunt Ruth's calm nature, induced though it was, and the way she glided through her days as if they were fields to be gone out into with a purpose, unperturbed and having what I now know to be her own continual intimation of infinity.

As Rose walked down the hall toward Ephraim still lying on the floor, wondering how to catch him up underneath her arms and lift him without squeezing him to bruising, I saw the cat again, coming in the house, hugged next to my aunt's breast, everything looping back, circled and complete, definite. Rose, the woman at Ephraim's shoulder, was the one I would've located had I ranged looking from the beginning to the end and back around to the beginning of our long story.

nine

DR. WOODWARD WAS NO STRANGER TO ME, AL-
though to him, I was a stranger, and the kind he
found unendurably tedious, alive or dead. He had no memory
of my name or Ephraim's name from the difficult period after
his angioplasty, when several episodes such as the pharmacist's
being accused of poisoning him and one having to do with
Glenda's breasts caused the neurologist to be sent to evaluate
whether my husband's bizarre behavior was due to something
pathological, Alzheimer's or some form of it, or if it could be
attributed to his sensitivity to the anesthesia.

Particularly given the doctor's fixation on Glenda and the
amount of time I spent with him afterward, that this man
could look at our names with no twinge of recognition was a
feat of forgetfulness. Back when Ephraim had been lying
there, muttering in the bed behind us, I'd told him, Dr. Wood-

ward, that from my point of view, it made sense to consider simple disorientation.

"Surely," I'd said, "it can occur when a man whose last memory is of cleaning out a pigeon cage suddenly finds himself in a clockless, windowless room stacked to the rafters with loud mechanical metal things, with a nurse telling him he's been there for the two days since a vein on the back side of his heart choked on the clot it was trying to pass. Plus, my husband's fatigued, doped up. That makes the most sense, knowing him. Everything he's said and done is thoroughly unlike him, but it waited to begin after surgery."

"Nobody wants to admit their mate could be suffering from any kind of dementia, especially Alzheimer's," Dr. Woodward said. "Their first reaction's always denial, but you have to admit your husband's behavior is beyond a cause as minor as strange surroundings, even if you take into consideration that he may not have much experience outside his daily routine."

Glenda was in the room, and later when she told me responding wasn't worth it, I said, "I know, but what kind of sheltered, elderly ignorance is he referring to? I'm not in denial about Alzheimer's. Ephraim and I've been on the lookout for it since they started making such a publicized hoopla about it. I've seen nothing. We spend every hour of the day together, so it gives us plenty of time to sit around and pick signs of craziness off one another, you know, just for the hell of it."

The belligerence didn't ring a bell, maybe because it was part of his daily routine, and although he thought about another of Ephraim's chief odd behaviors several times a day, he'd also divorced personalities from the incident he'd witnessed, remembering only how soft and round Glenda's breasts must've felt when the old man drove his face into them. Glenda also remembered and smiled when the scene passed through her mind.

She was on the phone with Rose and glancing out of her office every few minutes to wave onlookers away from Ephraim when Dr. Woodward snatched the chart out of the holder beside my door and went in, ignoring the curled body on the floor, telling himself, "Mother of God, you'd be an idiot to get involved with it. Leave it. Do this woman in five, six minutes; bill an hour, two; hope Glenda's working today; hope she comes in and shows me her big titties."

Ephraim's oddest behavior after the angioplasty had to do with Glenda's chest. Just as I finished explaining to Dr. Woodward why whatever was happening with Ephraim was fleeting, asking him to consider whether he could be overmedicated, Glenda was across the room, by the side of his bed, partially holding him upright and pushing pillows behind his back to brace him, agreeing with what I was saying at every turn. She needed help with his other arm, and as the doctor stood there, just as I reached the bed, Ephraim bolted up, rammed his face into her chest, shook his head vigorously and moaned like something wild struggling against suffocation. With Dr. Woodward looking at me to respond, I laughed, saying, "Mine are bigger, I think, from more use."

Looking through my records now and seeing that I was only an old local woman with no interesting bad habits, whose body would no doubt be claimed by a son or husband who'd call me "Mama," Dr. Woodward didn't anticipate anyone disputing the findings he was about to make without touching me. There were a dozen justifications he could've listed if someone had asked him to explain why women like me repelled him, but mostly, he disliked putting his hands on us. He often wondered what the repercussions would be if he wrote, "Shriveled to death," on our mortality reports.

Noticing the drained saline bags, he thought of the years he'd spent the holidays in New York with his grandfather, who always took him to the basement of the Metropolitan Museum of Art the day after the Thanksgiving parade, not admitting his fear of crowds but claiming a kind of missionary pity for deflated balloon characters like Popeye and Olive Oyl as they were being laid off from the entertainment industry, he was told, until next time. Sprawled limp on the enormous floor and spread across with pleats and creases that came up high over his knees, they looked like my deflated body, but at least, he thought, they had seemed a treat to be around back then.

As far as Dr. Woodward was concerned, Katherine Keller Doyal had been old all her life. I'd whined for ice chips and warm blankets and been willfully ignorant. People, he thought, who go on about dying with dignity should be able to look at women like me and know that such a thing isn't possible. Leaving me in the hallway, Dr. Woodward used what force of air was left in him to shove my chart toward Glenda and say, "Call me when the one on the floor's ready to be disposed of."

Looking up toward Glenda from the floor beside Ephraim, holding a hand against his shoulder, Rose whispered hard, "Good deal that one's gone. I don't see how somebody you could diagnose as a Ted Bundy could get licensed to have his hands on people. He's the kind of man that ties you up and you-know-what's in the corner, but listen, Glenda, how am I supposed to get Mr. Doyal up? I see a pulse beat in the side of his neck, but it could be off. His wife was right, Glenda. He's not a bad-looking individual."

Ephraim opened his eyes to find a big-boned woman who fixed a face too close to him, and as he began looking frantically around for a quick and plain reason why he was there, Rose said, "You didn't fall, if that's why you're worried; and I'm going to do what I was told to do, as soon as I can figure out a way for you to get up without me breaking my back or yours. Give me some help in lifting you, and you can go on to be with your wife. She's waiting."

"You'll need to peel off me," Ephraim said, sitting up and then holding on to the edge of a chair to stand. Glenda stepped toward him just as he staggered back, and when she and Rose had him seated, he said, "Let me sit a minute, please, and somebody say if my son's been called."

Glenda apologized about having to leave a message and went to her office to call again, leaving Rose sitting deliberately silent beside him, believing that it was best that he cry. His plan was to get up and go to my room as soon as he was sure moving wouldn't cause heaving; and when Rose began shifting around in her chair, he reached over and lay a hand on her arm to still the massive flowers on her dress, saying, "Whoever you are, be decent, don't move near me."

"I won't," Rose said, "but your stomach would feel better if I got you something to have on it. Hold the fort and let me ramble."

Bending down, she went completely through her massive red purse more quietly than Ephraim would've credited her with being able to do; and when she offered him a wrapped pack of Saltines, he felt a little amazed and told her, "Thank you, my stomach's probably been after something. How'd they not get broken?"

"I'm one of these that's a genius on things like that." Rose handed him another pack, which he turned down, wiping the crumbs off his hands, standing with her beside him now. "I imagine you'd like somebody to call the funeral home for you."

"Yes," he said, looking hard at my door. "You know the one?"

"Morgan's," she said, "the only white one, unless you're carrying her to Atlanta."

He said, "No, we signed on here. What's your name? I'd meant to ask it and see what you're here for."

"Rose," she said, "Rose Callahan. Katy said to be here, and the rest of it I don't believe would ever be my place to tell you."

ten

LOOK AT YOU, KATY, SO PRETTILY PROPPED. ISN'T IT THE poem you like? Look at so-and-so's daughter, lying there, so prettily propped?

Yes, Ephraim. They ring the bells for John Whiteside's daughter, lying there so prettily propped. We're astonished to see her.

Do you know whether I'm remembering this, or is it the truth, happening now, Katy; is it real? It's too solid in here to be a dream, and I'm not sure whether to care. I don't want to care if it's real, but I have to, and it's pretty goddamn astonishing, frightening actually, baby, like we've left on a trip without paying the bills. We're liable to come home to our electricity turned off. It's worse than that, though. It feels old and embarrassing for me not to know. Is it Sunday yet or still Saturday? Tell me and let me start there.

Today's Saturday, Ephraim.

When?

Saturday. There, now you know something, but you want something else.

To get up into your hair. Who let it down for you? Can I crawl in? Can I be here a minute?

Glenda did, before, but I wish she'd come in and put it back up. It looks like old strumpet hair down. Women my age should keep their hair cut.

Your hair's always looked better cut long. But listen, Katy, and let me tell you.

Yes?

I can't do it. I can't manage. My insides are buzzing, like I'm on a vibration I can't crank down.

Then be closer. You're tired. We've both been misdirected off the axis. Are you going to take your shoes off? Which would be a stranger way to be found? With me with or without your shoes on?

Rose, this woman I just met, said she knows you. I think she'd beat me around the head and face with one. What does she want, Katy? Who is she?

She's going to the other side of the day, tell you what to do if you let her, be between you and Wyatt if it's necessary.

But she doesn't know him.

He's worked so hard to make sure nobody does, being told how to grieve by a stranger may suit him.

He's unkind, Katy, and I dread seeing him.

He'll behave better this time, coming afraid.

They want a baby.

I know.

There's a load of white laundry mildewing at home. Did you know it?

Yes, and I know you've considered throwing it away and buying more.

How many sets of towels does somebody need?

Enough to be civilized with, Ephraim, but this is one of the ridiculous rotating things you forget about and allow Rose to manage.

I thought you'd tell me I'd stay sane by working in a routine.

Daytime and night seem like enough routine to begin with. Keep up with day and night and sleeping, eating, walking.

Jumping.

I know.

Maybe the story on Rose is she'll kill me.

Hush and try to make something decent out of Wyatt coming. What good would you be to a baby if they had one now?

They'll bring the baby to visit, then take it and leave. I'd like to take you and leave, but the Georgia legislature outlawed hauling, you know, bodies in a private automobile. I'd rather have you home in the right bed.

I'm still here.

Not at home.

Yes, there.

But not to see or hear, not to goddamn listen to.

You won't be alone. You can have something keeping you so full continually, grief can't push through to take over.

Even if I could stand the noise, and the large kind of scenery Rose appears to carry around with her like a spare snack of crackers, it wouldn't be enough.

It'll be as awful as you can bear it.

Well, what's on her list of duties?

To keep this time from being too much. How old are you, anyway, how well?

Old, old, and not well at all.

And if you had to say, wouldn't you say you'd been punished enough, two hours was already too much?

I could use some relief, actually, and some rest.

And you're still on the edge of the day.

But how do I explain another woman to people?

Who's going to do anything but look at your practical method of living and be astonished at you so primly propped on a clean bed, not dying of starvation in filth?

Wyatt?

Your having a strong-armed redhead in the house whose origins you can't explain will be good for him.

Tell me you don't expect me to look at this as a sexy arrangement.

Are you up to it, Ephraim?

It's just that she seems so packed with a swarming some-thing, activity.

The help isn't only for you. Rose may already seem to be too full of life, but she needs more.

What does she do, sit home and eat cereal?

No. Notice her hands next time if you didn't, her fingers.

Without you, there can't be enough left over. I'll be going around less than slim.

You'll have more than enough. You always have. We weren't, aren't, two of these people who needed the other to complete them. I was all of my-self by the time I came by the mud hole and found you, already the whole piece of yourself.

How do you know she's not a con artist or a common sneak thief?

Did she say her name was Shelley Winters? This isn't a plot, Ephraim, on Saturday Night at the Movies.

But it could be a plainer plot, how am I supposed to know what's what?

Because I know, and that'll have to be sufficient, except to say I wouldn't be prone to mismanage what little's left.

I'll be with you directly?

Unless they've come out with a different calculation from the one that says you've got next-to-nothing left on the average life span.

Goddamn, Katy, I was thinking about it backward—how long I'll be made to stay, not how little I have left. It'd be prac-tical for me to stay here until Wyatt comes with Ann. I can sit up and can tell them from here, love one another and never miss this, then they'll close the door and I'll stay.

Rose was meant to keep you from giving in through any means of sur-render.

It looks like a worthless vocation for either one of us.

If you don't take care of yourself, you'll stop believing you took care of me. You'll look at your whipped self and not be able to believe you spent so much labor and love on me, and you know you did. I was so well-cared for, Ephraim.

Katy, kept so very, very well.

And you as well, as were we.

eleven

As ROSE OPENED THE FRONT DOOR AND HANDED
Ephraim the keys, she said, "If I were you, I'd finally
bathe for the day and let me sit down with the letter."

"What letter?" he asked.

"The one that makes sense," she said, "for a wife to leave
somebody who's suddenly in charge of a stranger who's asking
sudden questions after being in the automobile, able but sitting there mum all the way. It isn't my fault the girl over by the
funeral home was a nitwit. I tried to tell you to bring the sheet
home about Katy and get your son to fill it out. You know
what'll make you feel better?"

Halfway upstairs, he looked up, then down, and told her,
"Falling headfirst down this flight of stairs."

"No, listen," she said. "When the girl read the obituary
she'd just typed out back to us, Katy sounded flat because of

the girl's tone, but picture different people reading it in the paper tomorrow, with their different afflections, and she'll sound more like the person they've known, not a blank stranger with a pet hobby of outdoor shopping."

"This is too tiring," he said.

"Well," she said, "your wife thought it would be, so I'm here."

"But why," he asked, "does it seem like the stupidest thing I've ever allowed to happen, particularly when Katy has shoals of friends who'll be here directly?"

"I don't know," she said, opening the drawers in the front hall bureau and moving the top papers around with her hands, "and I don't know where your wife put the letter, and I don't have time to mox through everything and get the silver polished, everything put up, cleaned, things of that nature. You have an idea where she would've put it?"

Seeing me again the morning he walked across the living room, asking why I'd slept so fitfully; seeing my hand by a cabinet, he said, "Oh, that's where she was standing, I think, but it wasn't like her to write up some letter pertaining to me. You need to let me read through it."

"If it pertains to you," she said, "then you should have the contents down, but I'd take a bath and get pointed more toward your son and his wife coming. You going to talk to them when they get here, or lay it off to me or Glenda, if she's off work and here? How long can you generally postpone it? But I can see why, on account of he in particular sounds like he may be one of these."

"That's something to say about a person you just met over the telephone," he said, "talking about nothing more than the airport."

"But probably," she said, "if it'd been me getting a collect call from a stranger at a funeral home about his mother's arrangements his father's afraid he'll fight with him over, I would've sounded irked as he did, too. What doesn't add up, though, is how neither one of you add up to sounding like him. He sounds northern. Is he adopted?"

He didn't answer. He pulled himself up the last few stairs, went to our bathroom, stripped, and rested his head on the faucet, staring at the water pouring with a strength that caused him to mumble, "Goddamn, wish I had it all or none. Some power's just enough to stop me." As he got from one through to 1:30, Rose sat in the kitchen, reading—

December 24, 1998

Dear Rose,

First of all, let me tell you I'm not feeling well and where to find Ephraim's Christmas present should this headache turn out to be something more than just what kept me up all last evening. Look under the bed in what's obviously Wyatt's old room, and there are seven or eight boxes I pushed under there and now can't get back under to pull out, anyway. They're his. You won't have a Christmas tree to take apart, as we decided we didn't want to put one up and have to take it down this year.

Now let me explain what I didn't. Anyone who doesn't know Ephraim well, which includes everyone, as we've always been private people, has no idea how deeply he dislikes jolts and threatening movements, physical or emotional. Torture can qualify as anything from Robert Mitchum lurking. He's honest, you see, in a way which has him believe he's being told the truth at every turn by every form of being, and trusts that what's advertised to be around a corner will be there. Maybe his years of working with the railroad and seeing tracks laid so plainly out along set routes; or maybe the army, which he won't say too much about; or his temperamental heart, which was injured by a fever, kept him in constant notice of this trait. He isn't a frightened person, though, or a guarded one, just watchful to keep the safety he's built for us in place. When we go to Las Vegas, for instance, we take what we're willing to lose.

He doesn't believe in ghosts or haunted houses, Ouija boards, talking animals, or any of the folkish claims of an afterlife, so if his take on what has become of me seems dry, it is. You'll note that I didn't ask anything strange such as your birthday so as to imply some unrealistic transition in your appearance and my departure, and you'll also note that while there are 300 or 400 books in the house, only one is a Bible. All of which is to say, Ephraim isn't going to be looking for me in clouds or banging windows, and if you entertain any superstitions of the sort, if you share them, I'm afraid it'll quite scare the pure living hell out of him. Just know if he ever says he sees me, it's memory; or if he's saying it while he's hospitalized, sick, it's probably morphine.

The friends and neighbors who'll come around to offer help are self-explanatory individuals and don't require illumination, which is not to say they're simple. We haven't made a habit of accumulating people who don't wish us well, so while they may not be as direct as you'd have them be, any questions they'll have about your sudden position in Ephraim's life will be coming from a genuine concern. Also, we never associated ourselves so intimately with another couple and had the kind of "couple-love" romance that draws some people together to the extent they eat, drink, travel, and so forth like four-of-a-kind, so there won't be an old pair who report after the funeral to attach themselves to Ephraim or invite you to jump in where I left off. We never had a Fred and Ethel. What I'm trying to say is we doted on one another to the fair exclusion of others, and there isn't another closeness you should feel obligated to maintain.

We did enjoy the company of several couples traveling around the north of England when we were there for Ephraim's army reunion and have kept up a regular correspondence——their addresses and all the other long-distance ones are in the small blue notebook in the rolltop desk drawer. If you could use my good note cards to write the thirty or so people listed, just a few lines about everything, it would relieve Ephraim of the burden. Between the Atlanta paper and word of mouth, anyone listed in the red book will hear, people, in the main, from the railroad, students and teachers I knew at Rome High School, other librarians in the state association.

While we're at the desk, also know something important——the owner of Morgan's Funeral Home has had every arrangement outlined and paid for since he ran a pre-need special several years ago. It's all receipted and filed in the desk, so if he begins to dither, claiming not to know whether some portion of the services is covered, the thorough lists and canceled checks will be adequate proof of my wishes. This is interesting——I read a book you'd enjoy called The American Way of Death, which is on the shelves in the wide downstairs hall, and learned how profoundly the funeral industry has manipulated our perception of what qualifies as mortal decency and how Mr. Morgan profits from what's more or less a heartless racket, running it like the company stores you probably remember from childhood, where farm or mill workers were forced to shop for marked-up merchandise, gouged, because that was the only avenue available.

After I read the book, I realized that the last and only avenue available led to Mr. Morgan's brick colonial funeral home, and I suggested to Ephraim that we locate a thrifty burial society and sign on for cremation or, at the most, arrange for two pine boxes, but he considered it a vile, miserly prospect. Instead, we became expensively involved with disregarding common sense and outfitted an inevitable, natural cusp between this life and the next in a way I'm afraid will appear overwrought, you know, awful.

I can't go on to another topic without satisfying the urge to justify the general lines of Ephraim's thinking and some particulars of how they played out, as with the bronze casket, the hand-sewn feather pillow, and the snowy cotton lining fabric you'll no doubt rightly guess to be 500-thread count or better—maybe I can help you reconcile the apparent waste with the contrast of washed-out refrigerator bags you'll find on the drying rack, the store-brand canned goods, and the Tang, which Ephraim prefers to regular juice, although Wyatt balked at groceries like that, mortified as he was by small economies.

The story is Ephraim and I met with Mr. Morgan at his establishment, spent an hour there in the middle of a swirl of brochures that were thoroughly packed with flattering come-ons, and after the pitch, as we were leaving, I told Ephraim I couldn't spend more burying us than my father made in ten years of teaching, and I'd go to the library and research these burial societies I'd told him about. Once I tell you this, I can go on, so let me say it's something to put his voice on to play through my mind now, like an old record that keeps a constant attraction. Knowing there's not much time left to hear it shivers me worse than the air near these cold windows.

He said, "We're Katy and Ephraim, not rotting vegetables the grocer leaves in the alley for dogs. We've never skimped traveling. If we were on an ordinary trip and had to separate for some reason, I wouldn't allowance you a dollar to hire a lean-to in a homeless park and expect you to wait on me there. I'd be sure you had the luxury bed at the Ritz to wait in, wrapped around in silk, and so I hardly see how it's debatable, Katy, whether we eventually wait well-tended."

We didn't know embalming wasn't mandatory until we read it, and although we didn't want autopsies either, it seemed unavoidable when people died in the hospital, which carried a high probability given that neither of us had a wasting disease like cancer that involved long lingering at home. We were both subject to attacks, which generally involve rushed dramas instead of calm decisions to make a victim comfortable on the floor until she improves or dies there.

You should know this. The hospital we were always taken to would use an autopsy to release itself from liability, but when we spoke with Glenda, she said it wasn't unusual for her to intercede for families who didn't want it done, so we had her note our charts, conceding that we'd allow our decision to be reversed if something unusual or suspicious, you know, potentially murderous, required it. My understanding is that Jewish people automatically avoid this ordeal, violating the body or putting it on an absurd three-day view being a violation of their theories.

There isn't such a thing as a civil service, which is odd, seeing as how it's acceptable for the passage of marriage, so we chose a Unitarian minister, a high school friend of Wyatt's who he'll probably contact as soon as he hears from his father or Glenda. I know it seems that his father and I have had a history of casting critical glances at him long distance—a cause for sudden praise at this point may come off as a rarity I've had to scour my memory for and then exaggerate into substance. But when I think of our son, I recall his respect for our spiritual beliefs and his open expressions of awe that they didn't conform, despite his criticism of so much else. He knew we were taking him to church to make sure he was exposed and adequately informed, and after he left for school, he wrote to say he appreciated the right we'd said was his, to choose between the fervor of the community and the apathy of our household.

I've often thought he was grateful for what amounted to our agnosticism because it argued against the hard conviction that his parents were intellectually paralyzed. He'll call the minister right away and go over every detail of his officiating, knowing if the funeral director takes it upon himself and hires a random Baptist, neither he nor his father could endure a violent tirade hurled over across me. Nothing needs to be spoken of beyond love, no rough demands that upset people or make them confront their own inevitabilities—there's no sense in it.

When he and his father commence around the edges of one another, you'll notice how expert Ann has become at stepping between them, so you shouldn't need to. She understands that an unhappy son makes a detached, distracted husband, and if she detects your presence is guiding Ephraim to Wyatt, she's clever enough to follow the trail from her father-in-law's happiness to her own and side against her husband should he try to remove you. Wyatt stays convinced that humanity would suspend its normal doings just to stand around and laugh at him if he showed a natural human emotion, and given how instinctual it's become for him to behave as though he's being observed and measured out to be criticized, I don't know that he'll ever easily put his arms around a pleasure. Neither his father nor I were anything but affectionate in his presence, so the origin of the cold is a mys-

tery, but if you see the road he needs, I wish you'd use the strength of character I saw in your hands to grab him off the side and make him take it.

Let me go ahead and apologize for the times Wyatt's going to say you're there because you smelled money. Everyone will want to be the first to tell you Ephraim and I came into a great deal of it, and they'll probably hint that it's well monitored and by Satan that there's not a chance in hell of anyone but family reaping any kind of benefit should he go missing or be discovered at the foot of the stairs. If I were you, I'd get the household money from him by the week, and you can look in the bill folders and the brown notebook to see what's due when, who we trade with for groceries, dry cleaning, yard care, and things of that nature.

It occurs to me to say, if he begins going to bed in his clothes, I believe you should let it be a necessary concession to the blues. I know you'll find a lovely way of watching him without being strict or reducing his opinion of himself as a man. Make him eat, if you have to load all the tabletops with food for him to eat subconsciously, as he can overdose on prescriptions if his dosage and weight balance are off. I could describe symptoms to stay on the alert for, but it'd be better if Glenda explained the mechanics of his particular heart to you.

On food, I've thought about leaving recipes, but just serve him what he calls for. Your asking will appeal to him. I was going to talk about cleaning, but you already know, and I'm beginning to wonder if I wouldn't be better off trying to rest before daylight comes or, as I've said, before Ephraim comes in to see if my breathing bothered me out of bed again another evening.

Before I close, I want to say, don't worry that he'll forget to take care of you. It may take a few weeks for his head to be straight enough to consider practical things, so the enclosed check should compensate you, I hope, well enough that you'll be able to feel safe giving notice at your other jobs and comfortable here, trusted, trusting. As you'd say, let's hold the fort a minute. I'm tireder than I thought I was, feeling like I'd better lie down and leave the rest of these life matters to another woman, you, not one of these.

Take such good care,
Katy

twelve

WITHIN AN HOUR AFTER WORD BEGAN CIRCULATING that I'd been taken to the hospital in an ambulance again, people began trading versions of, "Ephraim Doyal will be evermore screwed if Katy dies this time. He'll kill himself outright or starve, whatever it takes to be along fairly quickly behind her."

What they'll say is anything but unfounded, as Ephraim has achieved a kind of fame for his incompetence with household things, based not on aptitude but on a firm and long-standing refusal to learn. With regard to food, by the time we married, I was accustomed to his habit of sitting at the kitchen table and waiting to be served, like a hobo who'd wandered onto the property. My mother let him know it wasn't something nice people did, but he was resistant to shifting away from the few memories he had of his father and his idea of what a man does, which came not only from the scant time with the father but also from hours in front of movies like the "Thin Man" series, which never featured a man getting his own breakfast. Also, you know, our time dictated to him—something in the unliberated time we were born into gave him permission to sit.

My mother spent a year in England after my father died, and many of the letters I wrote her favored young wives' pleas to Dear Abby—how to balance work and love and find the steady bliss she'd enjoyed for thirty years, how to avoid resenting Ephraim for his quiet refusal to hear me when I said I needed help with the house, how to accept the fact that he wasn't interested in reading and couldn't get through a caption in *National Geographic* without falling asleep, how to deepen both physical pleasure and the crust on a pound cake.

She was over there when Wyatt was born, as Aunt Ruth needed someone alert to interrupt the rest of the family's plans to lock her away, and not in a place, Mother wrote, "as upscale as where T. S. Eliot stuck his addled wife." I'd thought when I brought the baby home Ephraim would do something other than observe the grinding labor, but he didn't; and after he babysat one Saturday while I went to Atlanta before I lost my mind and for the uplift of a few new clothes, I couldn't consider it again. He threw away all the soiled diapers because he couldn't fathom them becoming clean again, telling me the baby had "destroyed" them. As the weeks passed and he continued to do nothing beyond reminding me not to trip when I got out of bed to heat a bottle, I pushed Wyatt's stroller downtown and sent my mother a desperate telegram. It said something on the order of, "He still won't help. At the end of my rope. What do I do?"

Years later, when Ephraim and I were in England for an army reunion, while he was at what amounted to a brawl they held to celebrate the twenty-fifth anniversary of Normandy, I stayed at my grandmother's house off Edgewater Road and read all the practice drafts of my mother's old letters while several young grandnieces, thorough strangers, hounded me for money—I supposed it was to have the few blank portions of themselves tattooed and pierced. My mother wasn't nonchalant about anything, so letters she mailed were always copied on watermarked paper after she'd gone through enough rough drafts to satisfy herself that she sounded composed.

Looking at the letters, how her writing moved from a hurried dash to something as regular in form as lessons in a Palmer penmanship book, it was clear that this kind of thoughtful care and the time she spent were intended to be just another of the thousand ways she proved her love, a slowed approach to communication that can include larger gifts than you'd think possible, something I trusted the similarly slowed nature of time after a death to show Wyatt what lasts and what's fleeting.

The letter she sent in response to the telegram had gone through, if she kept them all, four drafts, during which she moved from intemperance to the deliberate advice I received. I'd never seen her first reaction to my predicament with Ephraim, as she was beginning to think it through, saying,

You need to harden an attitude toward his recalcitrance and use it without thinking. If you tell him enough times you're rolling over away from him to rest because it's on you to feed a baby of an evening and a man of a morning, noon, and night, assuming you're still packing him a rounded meal for lunch, he'll get the picture. Or he won't. If you come in the house and find him at the table, reading the paper or staring at your bum the way he's content to, waiting on you for supper after you've been on your feet all day, dealing with frustrating illiterates, the situation may give you the moral right to accidentally scald him, but the marriage gives you nothing but the legal privilege to keep cooking and rolling over toward him.

By the time she wrote the version of the letter I received in Rome, she'd deliberated her way from urging me to express an impulsive wrath to reminding me that love was more urgent than laundry,

At least he's grateful, and he sits and does his waiting politely. He's the kind of man who merits help, and you've always known that, you've always wanted to help him. And remember, stupid means knowing better, while ignorance is not knowing. Ephraim has the kind of domestic helplessness that's so ingrained it couldn't be unlearned if you signed him up for househusband lessons with Betty Crocker. Just remember, Katy, he doesn't go to hurt you, and no one is going to criticize you for hiring a woman to come in and manage some of the physical labor. I'd be doing it if I were there, so the postal order I've enclosed is for you to spend buying peace of mind. When you roll over toward one another, Katy, let me tell you, of these dear evenings, besides times you've brought the baby to your bed to ease him, there's nothing large or important enough to belong between you.

She was able to tamp down the anger about Ephraim, as his domestic ignorance was so complete a component of his personality that it became another attribute he was known by, like his truthfulness or his ragged sex appeal; and his appreciation that his basic needs were met was just as singular a trait, how he was known. He frequently seemed astonished by daily activities he'd seen countless times before. Watching me make a bed, he was amazed that I could tell the difference between the top and bottom sheet. Seeing a shower door cloudy and then wiped clean again, he was amazed, as he'd say, "at you taking the fog off it." Watching me cook, he once said, "I'm in awe of how you put one food in the oven and have it come out entirely another."

Maybe we lived like people in another century, but the lopsided division of labor was a choice that suited us, and I was so remarkably compensated, after a while, that I ceased to notice. I began saying I could give a natural damn if it was called to my attention by Wyatt or Ann, a neighbor, a friend who'd see me at the grocery store and make a joke of asking whether Ephraim was already waiting at the table. Until we had a child who was strong-willed enough to make us doubt our ability to maintain authority, our sense of control and balance, of sheer proportion, was so adamant that had a tornado yanked the house out of the ground with us in it and plopped it down in another county, we would've opened the door and walked out onto the tilting porch, gotten a look at the state of things, and calmly decided what to do next.

When Wyatt moved, the certainty about ourselves returned, and although it wavered during Ephraim's illnesses, during our last two years, when he held me, we knew we were holding something wholly irreplaceable. I'd made a fair and honest exchange, our deal, and without Rose, there wouldn't have been anything left behind on my side of the balance but a sucking, draining sensation of absence and loss. A deal like ours requires some thought and planning to maintain, and I'm sure some people would say it represented nothing more than a form of mutual enslavement or that I prevented Ephraim from growing into his full potential, but a man with his degree of ineptitude about things like whether rice is bought in cans or jars or whether you can use Windex as a gargle doesn't comprehend liberation.

Around 1968 or 1970, when women were said to be burning their brassieres, he said, "If you go around without yours, I thought you said they tend to hurt. Is what the women hope they'll get worth being stretched in the chest to an aching?"

I'd said, "A male librarian, Ephraim, is automatically offered medical insurance when he's hired, and I had to work five years before they'd consent to half-ass include it as a benefit. I could've had brain surgery with what they charged us for the deductible, and maternity was out of the question, but the men who worked at the depository were having moles removed and capped teeth galore. Does that seem fair to you?"

"No," he'd said, "of course not, Katy, and I backed you up when you had to raise hell with them, but what does throwing your underclothes in a public trash barrel have to do with it?"

I then said, "It's a protest, Ephraim. They're trying to bring attention."

"I'd think they'd do better," he said, "if they brought less attention to how mannish they look. Jane Russell snatching her brassiere off would draw more of the right notice."

"What do you mean?"

"They'd listen to her," he said, "but Congress isn't going to listen to pushy women that favor Agnew in the face and middle."

I said, "So, if you didn't think I was attractive, you wouldn't listen to me? Suppose I took my brassiere off and waved it at you, saying I needed some kind of opportunity?"

"I'll give you an equal opportunity," he'd said, reaching behind me, unhooking my brassiere, pulling it from underneath my blouse and throwing it over the back of the sofa, "to exercise your female right to be on top."

Turning off the lights and the news, I came back to him, asking, "And I'll get what I want?"

"So long as you don't forget to bend down to me," he said, "and let me love you there, the place I know, there, love you there, come to me, here, let me love you here on the flesh of your neck. Aren't you glad we were born when we were?"

"Yes," I said, "I'm glad all the time, but why is it important to you right now, this minute?"

"Because," he'd said, taking my shoes off, unrolling my

stockings, "your mother would've been more modern and she would've told you to burn your brassiere and serve it to me for supper."

"But I wouldn't've burned it," I said, "and when have you known me to burn anything?"

"Never," he said, "though you're about to. Lean down here and give me the flesh of your neck, please, there, the cool place, Katy, in the shade of your face."

thirteen

FLYING TO GEORGIA, ONCE WYATT WAS THROUGH thanking Ann for agreeing to stay with him for at least the duration of the funeral and the amount of time it'd take to get his father adjusted to a different routine, he slipped back into himself, telling her, "I don't know why my mother allowed him to stay so domestically crippled. You've seen it. It's more like a paralysis—like their thinking, frozen. It's all so goddamn provincial."

Ann said, "I've heard it, Wyatt. I know you think you would've smothered if you'd had to stay there."

"I've never been able to convince you," he said, "of how little my father was able to understand."

"He'd understand," she said, "if I said I'd rather stay in a motel. He'd offer to pay or come check into the room next to me, knowing, he has to, how you're going to be a wad of nervous complaint. You need a focus, Wyatt, so anxiety doesn't take over."

He said, "Getting my mother buried without some catastrophe isn't enough?"

"And you're in charge," she said, "of making sure that goes well? You're the catastrophe everybody's waiting to happen. Don't you see it? You think you're coming in to take over because your father's foolish, and he's got to be dreading the fight he'll have to put up against you."

"If you think he's going to be in any shape to get this done," he said, "I don't know why people depend on your advice. What about afterward? Are you prepared to drug him and drag him to Florida or to leave him alone in the house?"

"If you can't calm down," she said, "before we get there, the afterward is going to be us going back to California, cut off from your father, cut off from mine. Can't you be civil? I'll give you credit for the half hour you can be decent before you run out of steam or give up because it hasn't gotten you what you wanted quickly enough."

"Suppose my father says he wants to stay there by himself," he said, "and nothing I, we, say can change it? I could show up and do everything to suit him, and after the funeral, he could very well shove us out of the house with everybody else he forces to leave."

"I can't do it for you," she said, "or I'd try. You have to, Wyatt. You have to do something about your father or we're never going to get our lives together."

After a while, he said, "I'm thinking I might miss my mother there."

"You will," she said, "most definitely, but if you can make yourself not hurt anybody, I'll be at your side."

After they'd landed and collected a car to drive the hour to Rome, as they turned off the interstate and passed the clot of motels there, Wyatt said, "Drive on or let you out here?"

"Drive on," Ann told him, "but the road goes both ways, and you know I'll take it back."

Wyatt thanked her, and then taking the road by the lake, then the next one that winds around to the intersection between our house and the funeral home downtown, he asked, "Where do you think she is? Would she still be at the hospital? Is he at home, you think?"

"I don't know," she said. "They're one place or the other. It doesn't sound like you're going to stay pulled together enough to make decisions about the funeral, much less your father. Have you called the minister yet?"

"Yes," he said, "before I left the house. A friend of my mother's or somebody from school, whoever it was I talked to this morning, Rose something, gave me his number."

Ann said, "It's good Ephraim's had someone there today. You didn't know her?"

"No," he said, "and the oddest thing, she asked when our plane was getting in, gave me a couple of phone numbers I asked her to look up, and then she blurted something about Saran Wrap. I think she said my mother was out of Saran Wrap and she wanted to know what kind we used."

Ann said, "Saran Wrap's its own brand of plastic, well, cover, I think, but I don't know if I've thought about there being different kinds of it. What'd she mean? What'd you tell her?"

"I told her I didn't know," Wyatt said, "and I knew less why it mattered. I imagine she was covering food people were bringing over, but people aren't coming to the house until after the funeral, so there wouldn't be dishes accumulating this soon."

Ann said, "So what'd you tell her?"

Distracted, slowing to find the driveway in the snow, he said, "Watch me put us in the ditch."

"We're here," Ann told him, "we're fine, but I want you to tell me what you said to this woman, Rose."

"Why," he asked, pulling behind Ephraim's car, "is what I said about Saran Wrap so important to you? I mean, I don't know one kind from another. I thought it was, like you said, it's own kind of, well, thing."

Opening her door, looking back toward him, she said, "I'm asking if you were nice to her, Wyatt. If you weren't, you need to start. I mean to tell you, it's going to start."

Wyatt said, "Hold on a minute, Ann, just listen. I can't go in right now, just come back, sit here a minute. I want to tell you something."

Mad because she couldn't expect some order of loving tribute or promise he could live up to, she sat in the car again and told him, "Make it quick. If your father hears us and looks out here, this'll look weird, you know, usual for us. It'll look like what it is, like you don't want to be around him."

Wyatt looked at the kitchen window over the azalea bushes, pointed to them, and said, "We were in there one night, Dad and I. Mother was in the hospital, and you'd gone back home, a couple of years ago. We were in the kitchen, by that window, talking about what to do for dinner, and he says he wants meat loaf. You know how he said it, said his taste was calling for meat loaf, and, well, I said we should go to a diner, but he said Mother had some hamburger in the freezer. He knew I couldn't make meat loaf, so he didn't ask me, and I knew he didn't know how, but part of me thought, well, maybe it's the one thing he can do, maybe he's watched Mother enough, maybe she taught him."

Ann asked, "Well, had she? Could he do it?"

"No," Wyatt said, "not even close. Watching him stare at that frozen meat was like watching a retarded kid with an algebra problem put in front of him, and he has to solve it, you know, because his life's depending on it."

"So you put the screws to your father over meat loaf," Ann said, "and made him feel like his life depended on doing it correctly in front of you. Wouldn't it have been better to laugh it off and take him to the damn diner? Couldn't you ever let a thing go and go on?"

"You don't understand," he said, "how determined he was to make it."

"So, what did he do?"

"He boiled it. I left the room," Wyatt said, "and when I came back, he'd thrown the frozen meat in a pot of water and turned the heat on it. He said the meat would form into a loaf better if he boiled it."

"What'd you do then?" Ann asked, "What'd you say?"

Wyatt said, "Nothing. I left. I went to the hospital and sat with Mother, and when I got back, he'd gone to bed and left the meat floating in the pot, you know, a sopping mess, and so I cleaned it up, and I've known since then exactly how worthless he'd be taking care of himself—and, you know, maybe dangerous."

"It also tells you," Ann said, "he'll go to bed hungry if he sets his mind to it, so let's go see him. If he was that baffled with her sick, how will he be with her gone?"

"Terrible," he said, "possibly already crazy, but he's surprised me before."

Ann said, "When? I thought most of your problem with him had to do with boring tedium and predictability, you know, like when he got the money and didn't do anything interesting with it, nothing grand, just some trips."

"He used to take her to the Ritz-Carlton," Wyatt said, "for no reason—I mean, no occasion. But the point is, I mean, why he could surprise you is, well, you've noticed his hands."

"Not except where they were bruised the last time he was in the hospital, when we had to talk to that arrogant doctor about the anesthesia burning his veins."

"You should've noticed his fingernails," Wyatt told her, picking up her hand to show her, "where they're ridged, deep, you know, corrugated, from malnourishment when he was a boy. And what I mean by the surprise, Ann, is a boy who starved, who barely finishes school and joins the army, fights for three years and doesn't win anything, isn't promoted, isn't wounded to speak of, comes back and works for the railroad, stubborn, with everybody flying, saves and invests with the guy downtown who wears his shirts gaping open over his stomach—that's not a man who surprises you. Know what I told him about his work one time, Ann, the time I decided to answer what he was trying to teach me about success?"

Still looking at him rubbing his thumb over the smooth surface of her nails, Ann said, "I don't know, Wyatt, not about this. I know you've said many things to him—too much, actually, or else you wouldn't feel like you have to sit in this car instead of walking into that house."

"Something from a poem," he said, "something asinine I read and couldn't wait to tell him. I told him, 'Success by industry alone is a peasant ideal.'"

"Wyatt," she said, lifting her hand from his, "you know I love you, but I hate being reminded you've been an asshole all your life. It makes me worry."

"But I was a boy," he told her.

"And a boy like that," Ann said, "will be a man like that, and it worries me to think you'll never surprise me."

fourteen

WYATT WAS TALL AND LEAN, LIKE HIS FATHER, AND despite the kind of shaggy, loping way they both moved, they couldn't have been called slouches. Their clothes hung on their frames nicely, though nothing looked ironed once it was on them. I enjoyed watching them together; there was a physical beauty in the view I didn't find elsewhere, and I'd tell myself that if they felt as good together as they looked, it probably would've overloaded the senses, so it was too much to ask for an invented excuse to justify how immediately they'd need to separate.

I spent more than I should've on Wyatt's clothes, partly because he demanded it, but also because of the way good clothing looked on him, and I knew he made an impression when he went out pulled together correctly. Before his first dressed dance in Atlanta, he told me he needed a dinner jacket, and after I'd searched all the rental places in Rome and told him I'd come up with nothing and would have to take him to Saks or the Parisian to look for one on sale, he said, "You were looking for a tuxedo, Mom. People in Rome don't know any better than to call a dinner jacket a tuxedo or a tux or a goddamn tuck. That's the problem."

I ended up buying what he wanted, and after he'd put it on for the party, as he was trying to escape from the house, I stopped him and had him stand for a picture with his father in front of the mantel. I had to stop before I took it though, couldn't get it done, after Ephraim mispronounced something having to do with the new camera, which Wyatt couldn't let slide any more than his father could miss the chance to say, "Don't correct me on a goddamn word. It's dishonorable, particularly when you try to make a fool out of your father when you're wearing a suit of clothes to a school dance better than the one he'll be buried in."

Ephraim couldn't understand why Wyatt's first impulse was not to do the right thing, why honor wasn't practiced thoughtlessly, and neither one of us could identify what we'd done to cause his resentment other than not being higher-toned people. Once he met some of the parents of the boys he began private school with, families with serious old money, he more or less said we shouldn't expect him home for major holidays any longer, as he'd be wintering, summering, generally hanging around in places where these families had second and third houses.

He didn't board at the school in Buckhead, the best section of Atlanta, but the nights he spent on the floor in friends' dormitory rooms there amounted to it. When we realized it'd been a couple of weeks since we'd last seen him, when he and his father had argued about the tour of Washington, D.C., we were planning for his summer vacation, we made him come home, bribed him to come so we could give him some pleasing news with the kind of ceremonial bang it deserved. We hadn't come into the money yet, you see—we'd borrowed, sheer anathema to us—but we'd done it, and after dinner, his father and I made a deal over telling him we'd just bought a vacation home at Stone Mountain, which he surmised to be the unair-conditioned shotgun house it was.

While hell was breaking loose, his father reminded him of the high tuition we were obliged to pay because he was too good for the only public school in Rome—and that he was so ashamed of his mother that when he went to the library he treated her like a stranger and glared. They went back and forth, resolving nothing, getting nowhere, especially not to Stone Mountain. When the money arrived, after he'd moved to college, he said, "It's too late to do me any good," but it did him a world of good.

Whether it was his hope to keep benefiting from the windfall or a new conviction to change, Ann wasn't sure what motivated Wyatt to slip his arm around his father's shoulder as the two of them walked through the front of the still house. Rose, who watched from the kitchen, thought he looked like the kind of son who understood what he needed to accomplish that day, telling herself, "It's a good job he's not facing a career in falsifying emotion, on account of he doesn't look to have the stamina to pull it off much longer, not with his father smart, and his wife, not with her watching his face for truth to chase across it."

She closed herself in the kitchen, not wanting to introduce herself into a scene that was already tilting, rickety. Wyatt and Ephraim sat beside one another, and as they were going through some practical matters, Wyatt said, "Well, do I need to get a suit cleaned for you? You need a new shirt, shoes, or anything? I can take you to get a haircut in the morning. Ann can stay and get things here arranged."

Ephraim nodded at Wyatt and then at Ann, sitting across from them, saying, "Thank you, but I think both are set fine, my hair, the house. It's all right."

Ann said, "Ephraim, this is unusual to be saying, but the house does look, well, better than I expected. It sort of smells like Clorox and roast beef, like when Katy was here. I was planning to come in and do, you know, anything I needed to, but it looks like her friends already came and took care of most everything."

"And the upstairs," Ephraim said, "is going to smell like her dusting powder to you, on account of Rose brought a small suitcase of clothes over but she forgot and left her hygiene objects—powder, perfume, and so forth—so I told her to borrow what she needed of Katy's. She didn't know the powder in the pink container was flavored strong as it is, and she had the room fairly fogged before she realized what she was doing, how high she had it smelling."

"What?" Wyatt asked. "Are you talking about the woman I spoke to earlier, who made me waste time listening to her worrying about Mother being out of plastic wrap?"

"It was another kind she needed," Ephraim said, "and I took her to the grocery store to get some, so that's done, but Wyatt, I swear before God, you'd better not say a hard word to the woman. When you get upstairs, I'll be behind you, daring you to show yourself when you smell your mother's powder and say something about another woman invading."

When Wyatt asked why the powder was an issue, what that had to do with anything on the day his mother had died, Ephraim said, "The point is I'm trying to tell you something about Rose's character. I don't think she's used to nice things, and it's going to take some time for her to learn how to handle something that isn't watered down, you know, what she had to get cheap, a great deal of talcum, probably, with a small bit of scent mixed in it. She put a finger through a pair of stockings, and I said it isn't a reason to be embarrassed, but she said it wasn't embarrassment, just a difference she wasn't used to between rubberized hose from the grocery store and the silk ones of Katy's. It brought me back to being broke, when your mother cut the legs out of runned stockings to make another pair to last her."

Wyatt interrupted, almost shouting, asking, "A woman's here, wearing Mother's stockings and powder, so who is she?"

"It'd be hard to say who she is," he said, not appearing to care whether Wyatt required a better answer.

Ann said, "But, Ephraim, I think we'd both like you to try."

"She's not Katy," Ephraim said, "if that's what you're asking, not something I lost my reason and made up into life."

When Wyatt said he and Ann had figured that out, Ephraim said, "Well, good for you, because I hadn't. I had no way to know, until she put the powder on and didn't smell blue, whether it was Katy who'd found a way to come through."

Ann was worried that shock had allowed senility in, but when she asked Ephraim to explain what he meant, Wyatt answered instead, looking at the floor, telling her, "He meant Mother smelled blue after she bathed and dusted, you know, with the powder."

Ann said, "Blue?"

"There isn't another way to say it," he said, looking at her now, "just blue."

fifteen

AS IT OFTEN IS WHEN MEMORY'S WORKING AND everyone knows it and is staying quiet and still for it to work, the time is interrupted, and we're jerked out of the past and thrown, left to scramble until the next memory comes with contentment, uprooted, as in the tornado I'd imagine tearing our house out of the ground and throwing us down somewhere unfamiliar. Ann had just remembered the odor of blue, and Rose was in the kitchen, breading turkey cutlets and wondering whether to tape a note to the door, asking people to hold their casseroles for a day to allow Ephraim to rest. Just as she stopped working to smell her shoulder, telling herself she was scented pink, saying aloud, "I bet she smelled a beautiful blue when she dusted herself with the powder, smelled like the hospital that day, though," Mr. Morgan knocked once and let himself into the house, saying,

"Sorry to bother everybody, but I thought I'd better come in person. It's that kind of a problem."

Blue, pink, fogged dusting powder, memories accumulated and mixing in the air, were sucked out, leaving Ann, Wyatt, and Ephraim sitting in the vacuum, Rose holding on to the kitchen counter and frowning toward the door to listen better. Mr. Morgan was more bumptious in the room than he would've been had he been confident his news belonged in it, and though Ephraim indicated a comfortable chair, he sat in the only one that was too small for him, over by the desk, needing distance, Rose thought, as she heard him scraping it on the hardwood.

"This couldn't be good," she said to herself, wishing she had someone to listen now and tell her later she'd prophesied correctly. "It's about the body. It's something wrong with the body, and he can't fix it without their permission."

Ephraim said if he'd come for money, he could reach in the desk and find a receipt and the canceled check we'd made out to him over two years before, but he said, "No, it's not that, not entirely. You certainly paid for everything we receipted, but, you see, I didn't have a reason to look things over until, you know, we got her, and when I did, I noticed we didn't include a charge for the, you know, embalming, and I need to see about getting straight on that before we proceed with it."

"So it's the money," Ephraim said, already out of patience and without the will to hide it.

Mr. Morgan said, "I'm not asking for a payment now, no,

not at all, just, you know, the standard permission. I think the two of you went over the details with somebody else when you came in, and they just weren't as careful as they should've been, so I apologize for having to bother you now."

Ephraim said, "The man was careful. We were satisfied. When we went through everything with him, we just neither one of us called for embalming."

Mr. Morgan said, "Well, that could be true, but we need to go ahead and do that, Ephraim. You know, she'd want us to."

Wyatt and Ann started to speak, but Ephraim raised his hand and said, "Oh, hell no, she wouldn't."

"But I'm afraid," Mr. Morgan said, "you have to. I'm not in charge of these laws, Ephraim, and these days, with so many diseases and infections that didn't use to exist, they had to have something in the law to protect, you know, ground and water hygiene."

Wyatt spoke over his father's hand, saying, "I can't tolerate the ignorance. I can't do this. Do you hear how you sound?"

Ann said, "Wyatt, it's fine. It's not an emergency, not anything extreme, so let's talk about it and call Mr. Morgan later, if that's OK with Ephraim."

"What's OK with me," Ephraim said, "is not maiming Katy, and if you're going to tell me it's illegal, you know you'll be lying. If it's a thousand dollars you're hot not to pass up, I'll give you five to leave her alone."

Ann said, "He's right, Mr. Morgan. I read about what is and isn't legally required. Also, working with so many AIDS patients, I've learned that people can make this decision on their own. They just don't always realize it, and they certainly aren't told."

"We got it from the book Katy had, *The American Way of Death*," Ephraim said. "It's somewhere in the house if you want me to look up the topic."

As Wyatt was trying to remember another time his father had cited a book other than *Pigeons and How to Keep Them*, Mr. Morgan began explaining how not performing the procedure would create difficulties down the line. He said, "In some cases you take it in stride because it isn't a part of the individual's cultural custom, but you don't hear of that being the case in Rome."

Rose had listened, and now she was through listening, through breading chicken and ready to get in between Ephraim and the man. She pushed open the kitchen door, wiped her hands on her apron, and ignoring everyone in the living room except Mr. Morgan, she looked directly at him, saying, "May not be the case in Rome, unless you're Jewish."

She knew her appearance would startle words out of Wyatt and Ann, but she also realized they wouldn't stay silent long, so she spoke rapidly, with no space planned for argument, hoping they'd jump in and hang on to what she was trying to effect. Again, she said, "Unless you're Jewish, and then you have different rules, like you have to be buried by the next sunset and you can be left alone in the area of personal invasion, and Katy, with her family being Jewish but not practicing whole-hog, you know, full-out, she's entitled to have her wishes and desires obeyed."

When she had to take a breath, Mr. Morgan said, "Katy wasn't Jewish, was she?"

"If you know of her going to church," Rose said, "except when her son was growing up on account of the Protestant church was the only thing in Rome to expose him to, it'll be more of a hold-the-fort to me than you showing up wanting to violate her religion. I know her maiden name doesn't sound Jewish, but thinking like that gets people into prejudice, and I'm aware it isn't a rabbi sitting around in here consoling this evening, but the one she enjoyed the company of, you know, the intellect of the library and things of that nature they had in common together, he died some time ago, and you can bet he greeted Jesus unmolested. And if you don't mind me saying one other thing, if you didn't know her well enough to know her religion connection, don't you think it's a little nonchalant casual to call her by her first name?"

"I apologize for the familiarity," Mr. Morgan said, "and I should've realized something was up when I saw the hospital had waived the autopsy."

"We know a nurse that knows how to listen," Ephraim told him, "and I'm about ready to let this be the end of it and have you go on back downtown, knowing you listened and plan on respecting Katy's beliefs."

He said he'd gladly do what Mrs. Doyal wanted, and when he asked whether he could do anything to make the day easier, Rose said, "The day is what it is, Mr. Morgan, but let's let you out the door and have a better one tomorrow."

sixteen

THE SUN HAD GONE DOWN DURING HIS VISIT, BUT NO one had moved to put the lights on, so Rose went around and flipped switches, saying, "Tell me if it's too much. I know I dislike it turning dark so early in the winter. Daylight Saving Time's not natural. My family never changed the clocks, but that isn't what I went to tell you. I was trying to say I'm about to set the table and get some other things done, but I can stop and do something else if you need it. I don't know that Ephraim ought to be taking a drink of liquor, but we stopped over by the package store and picked up a bottle in case, sheerly on account of how it is that you never know when you're serving new individuals you don't know."

Wyatt said, "And it was you I spoke with this morning?"

"Yes, Rose Callahan," she said, "Rose. Nice to meet you. So, you want I should pour you a thumb, care for something to chase it with? It's out of season and high, but you can't turn Paul Newman and his lemonade down. I'll be sure to keep a juice on hand, with your father's health like it is and California. He wanted to get his regular Tang, but I told him he'll eventually parch his heart with the sodium count, and my experience with Californians is they go for things more natural."

Wyatt and Ann had been fixated on her, and though they had not sensed themselves sharing much lately, they suddenly felt a fast bond of staggering befuddlement, mumbling their thanks together. Deciding that the simplest way to get a simple answer about how Rose was transformed from a stranger to a stranger who'd dusted herself with his mother's powder would be to have his father narrate his day, including where she stepped in, with no reason for him to become defensive, concern but not in suspicious excess, Wyatt said, "This must've been a long day for you, Dad. All Ann and I had to do was sit on a plane and call the minister. I expected to get here and find, you know, what Mother called it, a running-around list, but like you said, you seem to have everything covered, down to putting on a fresh shirt and shaving, obviously nothing I've gotten around to yet."

He and Ann leaned forward as Ephraim began to answer, hoping the nearness would diminish Rose's large presence and allow them to hear him better through the racket that seemed to be coming through the air vaguely, off her loud hair and clothes. She stood behind the wingback chair near the kitchen, holding a dish towel, propped against the wall, telling herself, "Listening this minute, the boy doesn't sound half as incontent as you'd expect him to be, snobbish pair of school glasses on, hair too long and healthy-looking for a man, distracting the eyes off the thinned spot, one of these that acts like a tourist except when he's by himself at home, but his tone isn't his, more like Charlie McCarthy talking."

Ephraim nodded toward her and told them, "She and I, we left the hospital and went to the funeral home and talked over the obituary with a girl who didn't seem bright enough to write Katy up, least not to me. She seem that way to you, Rose?"

"As dumb as they get," Rose said, "and allowed to operate a vehicle and vote, depresses me, and I could run her down through the rest of the evening, but I need to see to things in the kitchen."

Ephraim thanked her, and when she left, he said, "OK, then, so she and I, we left the hospital and went to the funeral home, came home from there, and I bathed and looked after some matters while she took an inventory in the kitchen, and after she was oriented, we went to the grocery store, stopped by the package store and over by Sears to see about a pair of black shoes. We came back here, and she got herself organized in the guest bedroom and started supper, and I made some calls on the long-distance telephone."

Wyatt interrupted him, saying, "Is this shock? I mean, have you cried?"

"Cried," Ephraim told him, "and slid on the floor to lay there sleeping when standing wasn't happening to me. I did finally, and then I went in and stayed with your mother, sat by her visiting and had everything sorted out after a while. The difference between what you see and what you believed you'd see is I don't see this as the end, just an interruption that may last a week or a year, though if it has to be in the range of years, I wouldn't guess it'd be much longer than one, two at the most. You know, if you count the time I spent at Katy's parents' house, when my mother died and we were both fifteen, that's a long span of time, and if I have to be away from her now, in the scheme of history, it amounts to no more than ten minutes. I'm glad to be here, be gladder to leave."

"But Rose," Wyatt said. "I need to know why she's here."

The stress of a confrontation with Wyatt grabbed at the muscles behind Ephraim's ribs and shot a wet pain through his shoulder. With his voice crumbling into heavy pieces that wouldn't rise easily from the bottom of his chest, he coughed and then labored to whisper, "She's here because she was there. Katy would have to tell you the rest of it. I think I need to be quiet a minute."

He knew Wyatt wouldn't give him a minute more than a minute, and as a harsh acid flooded back up through his throat, scalding his gums, he realized his time was up and feared that everything he'd ever swallowed would spew across the floor if Wyatt kept squeezing. Ann spoke before Wyatt could, saying, "You look pale, Ephraim. Have you taken your medicine today? Blood pressure OK?"

"Glenda," he said, "took it this morning, said it was higher on one side and sent a cuff and another couple of scripts home with us."

Wyatt said, "Home with us? Am I hearing you right? Is she staying here?"

When Ephraim nodded, Wyatt all but shouted, "Did you hear how loud she is? How will you be able to stand it?"

"She looks loud is all," Ephraim answered. "I wish you'd stop sounding like everything's at the end of a rope."

When Wyatt said he was only trying to determine whether Rose was a hired woman and if she clearly understood whatever arrangement had been made, what her duties were, Ephraim said, "I can't guarantee she'll stay in her place, but you already saw a benefit of her deciding not to."

"But," Wyatt said, "you know I'll talk to whoever you need me to."

Ephraim said, "I didn't see you jumping between your mother and the table in Morgan's basement."

"OK," Wyatt said, "but what're you paying her to barge in and lie for you? Is there something in writing? You know, if she hurts herself here, everything you have could be exposed. It isn't like you to be careless about liabilities, and I'm sorry, but it's not like you and Mother to know, well, that many common people. I know you didn't socialize that much when I was living here, but the people I remember the two of you being comfortable with were, you know, better."

"A better class of people," Ephraim said, "a great deal better, actually, than me, and it didn't matter to me, but, son, this does—I despised the woman this morning, and even though it was a passing thing and had more to do with knowing she was meant to keep me from crawling in a hole I already had an eye on, what I'm trying to tell you is not wanting her around has been done, and you don't have to do it. She doesn't need it accomplished twice. Nobody sane would call for a second whipping by an expert, and I don't call to be treated like I was so disdone I picked up a dangerous stranger off the side of the highway this morning. Her way of putting herself and what she picks to call jewelry irritates you, but you'll ignore the sound it makes when you decide to stomp damage through here."

Wyatt looked to Ann, saying, "Here we are again. I try to offer a way of thinking about things, you know, in case this woman's some kind of con artist, and he turns it around."

"The way you generally offer," Ephraim said, "all it involves is blowing in here and showing yourself."

Wyatt said, "This didn't start when I moved. I can't remember the last time I did anything right in this house or when I've known what you wanted."

"He wants the same thing I've wanted from you," Ann said, "the thing we both dread wanting perpetually."

He said, "And you both make me guess at the mystery."

"No, we don't," she said. "What we want couldn't be simpler. We want you to surprise us, Wyatt. We need you to come outside of yourself long enough to surprise us."

seventeen

WYATT KNEW HE HAD TO SUPPLY A BENEFICIAL surprise sooner rather than later, so rather than acknowledge Rose was human by eating the supper she'd made, without saying where he was going, he got up from the table and left the house. Rose said, "Is that normal for him or abnormal?"

"Hard to say," Ann said. "They run together. I've lost the ability to tell."

"And the will," Ephraim said. "Sounds like it, but somebody that jumps and runs like that, they need to do something right now or go off to think, so I wouldn't chase him or hound him back on his cellular telephone. He'll slip in eventually or come banging, depending on whether he's accomplished what was his aim. He did something like this in school, when he couldn't find the nerve to ask a girl to a dance, so after he'd put it off and put it off, he went out of here like a shot one evening and ran three, four miles to her house, and from what her mother told Katy, got there, falling in the door, sweating, drunk, they figured, which of course he wasn't."

Ann looked at her plate, aggrieved not to have seen the force of passion, and after Rose looked hard enough at Ephraim to let him know he'd finished the story in a sorry place, and he needed to furnish a better conclusion, he put his hand on hers and said, "He didn't have a driving license is why he went on foot."

"Running," she said.

"Just nerves taking over," he said, "first date, and then the girl turned him down to his face. He didn't run, he walked—drooped—the whole way back, climbed in his bedroom window after dark, shamed."

Rose said, "He's gone to see a man about a dog is all." Ann didn't understand, so Rose continued, "It's what somebody, particular a man, likes to say when he's on his way out to do something for you. They don't tend to use it to cry wolf with or use to cover over affairs because if they've been at the hard end of a fight before they went out, they want you to spend the time they're gone anticipating and improving your mood so they don't have to worry about walking in to more of the same. He's gone to do something for you, believe me, a surprise."

"But the stores around here," Ann said, "close in less than an hour, and it's certainly not enough time to get to Phipp's Plaza or somewhere like that in Atlanta."

Ephraim said, "Anything he'd get you in Rome, it'd be a holding present."

"That's right," Rose said, "something to tide you over until the Parisian or Neiman Marcus opens, so if he comes back with something he's blown through Sears Roebuck and grabbed, even if it's a set of drill bits or a pair of Wolverines, I'd let it be fine and say he did what he was able. And I'd also be looking forward to when Ephraim gives you whatever it is he's picked out of the jewelry box here for you."

Squeezing his hand, Ann said, "You didn't need to do that."

He hoped he wasn't thinking, "And I didn't," loudly enough for her to hear it, and when fear of forgetting mixed with the sadness in Ann's eyes, he stood up and kissed the top of her hair, saying, "I need to go see a man about a dog myself. The pen's upstairs, though, so I'll be back long before directly, before, I'd think, he gets back with the bit set and brogans for you."

As they cleared the table, Ann asked if Rose had been a friend of Katy's. "I know her family's either passed away or still living in England," Ann said, "and except for the people they met when they went overseas for Ephraim's reunion trips, I don't think I ever heard her mention, you know, going shopping in Atlanta, out to dinner, doing social things with other women; but we also didn't talk that much—well, that intimately—so I'm certain there's a lot I don't know. I hope you don't think I'm prying, though, or suspicious. Wyatt can hold down that end of things. I don't know if I have the energy."

"You look tired in the face," Rose said, "and you don't know from prying."

"What do you mean?" Ann asked.

"I was thinking about asking you if you're expecting," she said, "but I won't, so just disregard it, and for the other, no, Katy and I became friends only at the very end, the very, very, but between talking to her a long time at the hospital and the letter she left me, I know her fairly well, at least well enough to know she's like me and not one of these. In fact, I believe I'm going to get ready and ride over to the funeral home and see if they'll let me set up with her."

"Well," Ann said, "I don't know how long Wyatt's going to be gone. I could go with you. Should I see if Ephraim wants to go?"

"Sure," Rose said, "if you'll go finish cleaning off the table, I'll throw these last few things in the thing and go in there and holler up the stairs at him."

Ann had never seen a woman move with such sharp speed in a kitchen, and before she knew it, Rose was standing at the foot of the stairs, shouting upward, "You can finish rambling through the jewelry box when we get back! If you feel up to getting a coat on and coming on, I'll ride us downtown to set by Katy awhile."

He appeared there. Rose saw him and worried that he was about to tumble down the staircase, and as she rushed to him, she called back to Ann, "Grab him a glass of cold water, and run open the cabinet by the refrigerator and bring the blood pressure pills."

"Which ones are they?" Ann cried out.

"I marked the bottles with a magic marker," she said, "big letters, plain. Panic'll blind you, so get them, Ann, hurry on."

The three of them were arranged around the top couple of steps, trying to make Ephraim tell them something besides that he had no idea, when they asked, why his pressure had so suddenly dropped. When he was able to stand and stubbornly claim himself ready to go to the funeral home, the front door opened to Wyatt stepping in the foyer, mumbling, "God-damn, it's cold, forgot Georgia can get this damn cold. Who's up there arguing? Why's Dad yelling?"

To see him without stooping, Ann came halfway down the steps, looking for a bag in his hands or lying by the coat he'd just thrown across the wide foyer table. "Your father," she said, "just had an episode, something with his blood pressure. He's better now, but he shouldn't go out in the freezing air."

"Why," he asked, "would he want to go outside?"

"Sorry," she said, "looking for the dog distracted me, but, well, we were going to go to the funeral home and sit with your mother awhile. I thought it was a little late, but Rose said they allow families in, you know, after hours."

Wyatt smiled and turned on switches by the door until he found the ones that lit the porch and the lamp by our curb, saying, "Hold on. I told the boy the house numbers are hard to read, so I'd leave these lights on. Listen, about my mother, the funeral home—you don't need to fight my father over staying home. They'll be here in a few minutes with her."

"Wait," Ann said, "is that the surprise?"

As Rose helped Ephraim down the last steps, everything she had to say out loud joined with everything Ann had to say, and Wyatt, still smiling, heard nothing but addled talk of an odd gift and strange consideration, a grave-robbing prodigal, the way things used to be, but through it, above the words, like a gift of its own being lifted up out of his frustrating clot of inabilities, his father said, "Very good, son, thank you—very good, son, to bring your mother to us. She'll be well looked-after, very well. Very good, son, I thank you."

eighteen

"ANYBODY CARE FOR A SNACK OF LATE SUPPER?" Rose asked. "You didn't eat, Wyatt. Let me fix you a plate."

"No," he said, "I hadn't yelled at the clown in a long time, so I went by the Circus drive-through on the way there, to the funeral home."

"Well," Rose said, "I'm glad that's decided and we can go back to sitting around in here, nobody saying anything, which is beginning to wear on me, so I'm going to go on and say good night. I'll come down later and stay with her."

The boys from Morgan's had placed the bronze casket on a low riser in front of the fireplace, and while Ann and Wyatt could look at it only intermittently, Ephraim stared at it full-time. After Rose was gone awhile, he said, "Can somebody look in the *TV Guide*, see if something's coming on? I've seen this string of *Law and Order* reruns so many times I started feeling guilty of the crimes."

He was in an overstuffed floral chair nearer to the casket than Wyatt and Ann, who were together on the sofa, both wondering when the conversation about whether his bringing me home, a decent and moreover kind act, was the kind of surprise she'd had in mind or whether she was holding out and planning to hold out for something thoughtful, tangible, and right. Finding the day's listings, Ann said, "We could watch *Who's Afraid of Virginia Woolf.* I haven't seen that lately."

"I have," Ephraim said, "I and Katy tried to watch it to the end not too long ago, and it scared her as rotten as it did the last time, so we had to give up trying."

"I know," Ann said, "they're cruel, you know. They know just where to push, psychological torture."

Wyatt said, "Argument scared her, and anything unpredictable, sudden movements. She disliked watching fireworks that didn't go off, you know, regularly. She stopped going down to the river to see them. Remember that, Dad?"

"I do," he said, "but it was she preferred things happening naturally but in order. Neither one of us appreciated somebody in a fright mask jumping out, but her issue was more wanting time to think about a thing before it happened. When the investments came through, it took a week or more to get over the unexpectation for her to pay attention to what good it could do us."

Wyatt said, "So, Dad, doesn't that make you wonder how she'd feel about Rose?"

"She'd feel," Ephraim said, "terrible about how you feel about her, how proud you'd be if she was colored in a uniform."

Ann said, "I haven't been in the mood to defend him lately, but I think it's standard behavior for any son to worry about his mother being replaced, and with her here so soon, you know, the potential for some involvement."

Rubbing his face hard all over, Ephraim said, "I knew this was going to come up and crawl over me like a goddamn itch. This isn't anybody's business but hers, but she told me today she dropped her interest in going out on dates soon after she had her hysterectomy out. The fact is somebody trying to be sexy around here isn't a consideration. You believe she's after money, and what she'd get would leave less for you."

Ann knew the presence of a casket wouldn't keep things from going absurdly and rapidly downhill if she didn't stopper Wyatt's antsy and self-delusional convictions about the rewards he deserved for having been born to average people who didn't stay amazed at the level of intelligent sophistication he'd been forced to claw himself to. Futile as she realized it was to mention Florida, she needed something to shove like a large boot between the two. "So, Ephraim," she said, "I was wondering if you've given any more thought to moving to Florida, because, I mean, there wouldn't be an issue with Rose there, because, well, you'd be living with us, and we'd all be near my parents, and if everything works out, there'd be a grandchild, so some of the tension about caregiving, money, well, I think a great deal of it actually would abate."

After Ephraim didn't answer, Wyatt asked whether he planned to. Shaking his head and focusing on the casket again, Ephraim said, "Nothing to say but I'm planning to live my life as is, and none of this other's in it."

"You want to live your life," Wyatt said, "like Mother's still in it. Rose is here to make you feel more like nothing happened. You wouldn't last in an empty house, and that's fine, but I don't know why you can't admit you hired her, you know, to be here."

"What of it," Ephraim said, "and so it's so? Isn't it my business and your mother's?"

"Not if you're trying to avoid facing reality," he said.

Ephraim said, "And if that's what I was doing, it's mine to avoid, but whether I escape or wallow isn't your concern."

"Something's bound to go wrong," Ann said, "if you try to make Katy present here, that's all."

When Wyatt lay his hand on her knee to compliment her logic, Ephraim said, "Wife says something you can use, you more or less throw her a bone, but you're the one who brought Katy here, why she's present."

"I thought you'd like it," he said, "and you wouldn't have to think about her by herself at Morgan's, and I thought it'd make it real."

"Oh," Ephraim said, "it's real without the object lesson,

but if your mother isn't overall here and present to you, casket or not, you knew her well enough to know what you're miss-ing."

Turning to Ann and beginning to cry, Wyatt said, "So you tell me, is he saying I should leave him alone and let him keep everything to himself?"

Ephraim said, "I'm out of tolerance. I'd rather write a check than be hounded to my own goddamn grave for it."

"I used to want the money," Wyatt said. "Thought it'd feel better if I got paid for constantly feeling like I was in the way, but now I know it wouldn't. I brought Mom back here to have us, you know, be three, but it's like it always was: the two of you and me. There're so many memories of me disappointing one of you, and one tells the other, then you both could go for days like I wasn't in the house."

Ephraim said, "I don't think that's so, Wyatt. You weren't excluded, but there were a great many times when you behaved like you'd like nothing better than go live in a motel room."

"Because," he said, "it was so goddamn uncomfortable, and knowing you had me late added to it. I mean, I didn't no-tice it so much at home, but when I'd see Mother at school, I saw how old she was."

"Well," Ephraim said, "what're you going to say when a child says something to you about having him old?"

Ephraim continued, "You're trying to think your mother and I had you by mistake and felt interrupted from being together, but that wasn't the case. Married people holding down two jobs and trying to save and being worried about a child needing something you couldn't pay for wasn't just invented."

When Wyatt moved to lay his head in Ann's lap, she gave him a pillow and pulled the blanket down from the back of the sofa, saying, "You assume so much, think so fast, so wrong sometimes, and you need not to, just need some rest, so I'm going to bed, and you should get settled here for a while, just stay with your mother, and, well, I don't know what to say but, be settled."

Wyatt thanked her, and while she bussed the room, straightening around in it—the way the last woman to leave one will instinctively do, and something my mother said distinguished girls from women—Wyatt, oblivious, said, "It's just a couple of my things, Ann. Leave it for Rose in the morning."

She ignored him, as did Ephraim, who stood and touched the cool bronze for the first time. Resting his hand there and looking at Ann using the hem of her long sweater to blot the circle she'd found under Wyatt's glass, he said, "Katy being sick, Ann, I missed your birthday, but when you go up there to bed, be sure not to knock what's under the pillow and have it roll off away from you across the floor."

"Ephraim," she said, "are you trying to say there's a ring under my pillow?"

He said, "I wanted you to be able to go to sleep with it on, the one I gave Katy when Wyatt was born."

When Ann left, Wyatt lay down and pulled the blanket up to his chest and commenced a full-out sobbing. She heard him from the bedroom, as did Ephraim, who'd eased away to bed, and while neither knew whether he was on the verge of another bout of temporary contrition or if the epiphany they'd waited for was coming, they were both certain that the duration of the night could be the difference between him waking into another solitary morning or awakening with them and whole.

nineteen

EPHRAIM HEARD NOISE IN ROSE'S ROOM AND knocked, asking if she had everything she needed. "You can crack the door," she said, "it's decent in here."

Startled into asking, he said, "You always crawl in with a full face on? Aren't you suppose to take it off?"

"With company in the house," she said, "I thought I might have to get up and tend to something, and I've got the clock set for five to go downstairs and set. I don't want people to wake up and face a haint."

"You don't think Katy's going to haint, do you? I hadn't thought about that."

"No," she said, "it'd be me the haint without a face on."

He said, "But are you wearing regular clothes, too?"

"Ready-to-roll," she said. "Just for this evening, though. I forgot my housecoat, need to run by my house to get it and bring a few other things over."

"Katy's got one," he said, "just take what you need, not a problem."

"I might later," she said, "but not while your family's in the house. No need to agitate and add to the stirring, but hold the fort and let me tell you, that was something he did, bringing his mother here to the house."

Ephraim said, "And you can bet I'll get a bill from the funeral home for the inconvenience, some way they'll turn it around to where I owe for her not being there, but it's worth about anything not to go to the place."

"I know," she said, "I always dread it, sharks and new haints shut up in a Civil War house with the old haints ranging around in the walls, hard to imagine something more made to scare the life out of you, but you don't have to stay up thinking about it now, so I wonder if you hadn't ought to try to get some rest in. I split your medicine and labeled it large in your cabinet to save you from saying it's too much trouble to go downstairs when you forgot it."

"How'd you know," he said, "I forgot it?"

"Because," she said, "you hadn't taken enough the past two weeks to keep a pigeon alive, and I forgot to tell you while you were bathing today, I went out there and fed them. Several, least to me, looked lousy. I can go over by the pet store for some delousing agent and fog the pen the first chance I'm able. My uncle had parakeets, thought they had dandruff, turned out to be a roaring case of lice, had to more or less scald it off them."

He said, "This is the very thing what people that's going to accuse us of taking up don't realize."

She said, "What are the people that's going to talk going to talk about? That I know from bird lice?"

"Yes," he said, "exactly, but it doesn't bother me. I think we understand one another."

"We speak the same language," she said, "like me and your wife, the three of us, none of us is, was, one of these that doesn't understand us."

"I know," he said, "and you made the day bearable, and I'm going to go lay down before my eyes close walking."

Ephraim also crawled in bed ready-to-roll, not out of convenience but to make him appear less like vulnerable prey when sixty-five-year-old memories of his mother's death and the treatment she endured in a nightmarish funeral parlor began lurking. He knew it was a perfect evening for torment, and as the scenes came forward, he realized that tricks were useless against them, so he got out of bed and took off his clothes, holding his trousers, remembering of the ones my father had bought him back when he'd been a little boy on the way to the funeral home where his mother lay, how kind my father'd been, and physically strong, it turned out, to be a bookish man, a scholar. In his pajamas now, and under the covers, the absence of weight on the other side of the bed maddened him when he rolled, missing the tug of a sheet stuck under me, so he got up again and pulled random thick books from the shelves and stacked them where I'd been, saying, "There, now, there, that's got it, there, but you know the ghoul that hurt Mama, he's still here, loves this kind of evening."

His memories of the funeral parlor hadn't been exaggerated by time and retelling. It was the absolutely gothic affair he was seeing. It had been torn down in 1970 and replaced by a grocery store, and we weren't the only people in Rome who boycotted shopping there or went very reluctantly, so many of us having heard tales or suffered experiences with loved ones that gave the preparation of the dead a bad name. Misery hung over the place and, odd to say, it remained over the A&P.

Mr. Morgan's father owned the other establishment, and when he sold out to become part of a conglomerate, a kind of chain, like Arby's or, well, the A&P, people regretted the demise of another family business, but as Ephraim said at one of the rare dinner parties we went to, "At least you know how the person you take there is going to be treated. They have a set of steady regulations, and it might be impersonal, you know, how these large funeral concerns run things like the automobile industry, but at least you don't have to trade with the hellhole they brought down where they put the A&P, and they may turn out an accidental lemon now and then, but I don't know that I've ever heard of a bruised and broken automobile coming off the assembly line in Michigan."

When my mother learned that Ephraim's mother had been taken to the hellhole, she told my father, "If you waste our savings or decide to scrimp and force me to be laid out in that filthy pile and allow that ghoul to put his claw hands to me, you won't be able to open a door or a book without me there, shouting, and sweetheart, it'll seem deadly real."

They were both so disturbed that my father called Mr. Morgan's grandfather and made arrangements for her. Then he took Ephraim to his tailor and had four new suits of clothes fitted for him and some of his own shoes and jackets reconditioned—an odd thing to do, I'd thought, on their way to the funeral homes. Until my mother happened to mention the tailor episode to me in one of her letters from England, I'd considered it only as another burst of my parents' impulsive generosity, but it was more, as I learned, as she said—

Remember the time your father got all the clothes for Ephraim when all he'd needed to get through his mother's funeral was a decent black suit and polished shoes at the most? It came back to me today when I took Aunt Ruth out shopping for a radio, the only thing she'd need that isn't furnished by the assisted-living facility. I'm so glad she's headed there instead of the horrifying institution everyone said she'd be fine in, not knowing the difference, dead to certain sensations, you see, just as Ephraim's mother was when her brothers and sisters wouldn't chip in to take her to Mr. Morgan's place. They no doubt enjoyed believing she didn't know how she was being treated, the way people here believe Ruth to be oblivious.

When I took Aunt Ruth around from one store to the other, pursued by boxes and wrapped packages I had delivered to her little room, with all her new, allegedly feebleminded housemates, curious and somewhat confused in the halls, I realized I'd gone out after only a portable radio and ended up with furnishings for a Taj Mahal—which immediately brought to mind Ephraim when his mother died. Your father and I saw the boy you'd always adored as a brother and had begun to love as a husband on the verge of the unknown, and it was overwhelming.

In Ruth's room, Katy, as she was setting up her housekeeping with all her new, interesting things, I could hear your father again, saying Ephraim was without a family except for us now, and he was going to see to it that the boy stop being discriminated against, as you know he was, because one look at him said he was as poor, well, as he was. His mother had been such a taker on the one hand and so proud on the other that we never knew if a pair of birthday pants were going to thrill the woman or cause her to strike out, hateful.

When the medical director of Ruth's new place stopped in and saw all her booty, from the satin curtain valences to the needlepoint carpet to a gorgeous tandem bicycle I couldn't resist and defended to the man as the perfect, well, vehicle for Ruth to use as she's trying to make friends, he said outright her local people had made no plans with him concerning her care, and they virtually slowed down driving by and dumped her off. I felt like I was finally doing something that counted, and I recalled how amazed Ephraim was that your father would take

the time to escort him on such a significant part of the
journey to manhood.

I believe he was even more grateful, that same day,
when your father went after the ghoul they found breaking his mother's arm. I said then Ephraim would be hard
pressed to go into another funeral home—he will always
have to suffer the memory of opening the door to the
sight of her being manhandled into her dress, despite the
fact that it had already been slit up the back with the pair
of long, brutal scissors the undertaker threatened to take
to your father, before he reversed the situation and beat
him, he said later, blurringly swiftly. Do you remember
being on the porch with me, as he carried Ephraim up
the steps in his arms, like a long-legged child, his telling
us he'd heard the bone snap? I remember you putting a
record on so he could hear something else, have his ears
full, you said to me.

Ruth may've had to endure a life with very few benefits of practical sense, and she's been repeatedly given to
know the world lacks patience for her, but you have to
hand it to the English and know when she passes, she'll
be cared for respectfully. You know, Katy, when the time
was, before, when we died in our homes, a woman would
come into the room, carrying a basin of warm water.
Rags torn from bird's-eye were soaked and then squeezed
over the basin so that water didn't chill on the skin or run
down and pool at the nape of the neck. Bloody water was
thrown into the edge of the winter woods or into a barren field, and the rags were burned.

And in a grieving house, Katy, if there were words spoken, they were spoken softly; people moved with care. I remember jerking a drawer open, you know, with the clang and clatter of the utensils, and having my grandmother tell me to go sit in this family's yard and develop restraint, not rudely, just firmly, to get the instruction in me. She was exceedingly sharp, though, when misbehavior wasn't accidental, and people weren't able to resist the urge to show themselves in front of an audience of mourners, like an insecure bride who can't control the urge to bring ugly attention to herself. The only loud sound she found tolerable was the howl of the wind blowing through bottle trees, catching evil spirits that were believed to enjoy a sympathetic attachment to good souls lately set loose in the air, and she had to accept it, couldn't wish it away because, she said, it was so darkly necessary.

They knew the order of nature, you see, so it was natural to follow it, to pour blood on barren and cold places as a kind of nourishment, to be respectful of the processes and procedures nature had laid out. The reason I know so much about this is that my mother's mother volunteered with a burial society, and when she lived with us, she'd go out on calls, taking us sometimes, but only to calm houses where the cause of death hadn't been violent. When I was about twelve, she became locally famous and was written up in the paper for instigating a kind of shunning. She arranged it so that a young woman in the community would no longer be permitted to attend to other women at their birthings, weddings, or deaths because she had begun singing "Yes Sir, That's My Baby" while helping wash her mother's body.

What she said to me about it was something like this—You must never forget that a whistling woman and a crying hen, neither shall come to a good end. Never act out of your nature. A bad woman who sings at the wrong time deserves the trouble she brings to herself. She could have a first child born to her with teeth in his head. Don't whistle, don't sing, don't be loud in the company of the dead, don't dip snuff, and don't wash your underthings with lye soap, or you will pay. Respect life. Respect death. Do the best you can in between.

I think what she did helped those left behind trust that life wouldn't deteriorate into the black chaos that they feared was waiting for them—at the end, Katy, I think everyone, no matter how religiously convinced they are of promises of gold-paved streets, angels, and so forth, is afraid that the truth of eternity involves nothing more glamorous than a big deep and empty hole. But let's hope it's closer to the version you talked about to me, after the baby came and you and Ephraim made out your wills, how infinity is made only of the chief emotions we felt in life. Not caring for the other definitions, your father and I talked about it and decided that your vision had our name on it, and I don't think I've told you this, but he and I borrowed our confidence in our infinities from you.

twenty

NOT ABLE TO SLEEP, WYATT THOUGHT, LEAVE THE lights on, I see her. Turn them off, she's still there. This was a stupid thing to do, bailing her out for them to approve.

It wasn't stupid, Wyatt, it was spontaneous, kind. Your father knows better, how you've felt, you know, like a third wheel, and Ann warmed up enough that moving upstairs would be a wise move, especially now that she's wearing the ring he gave me when you were born.

Hold on, is this thinking or being? Is it still right now or is this outside time?

All that matters is what's on your mind.

You mean, I can ask you things?

You always could.

So, if I ask if Ann loves me, you'd know?

I always did. The order of omniscience that allows a mother to see what exists between her son and the woman he's married and know whether it's real is, well, assigned long before we get here.

Where's here?

In love.

Is that a place?

It appears to be.

Are you OK?

Well, it's outstanding so far, an excellent seat.

Like at a play, having expensive seats? Are you up there with the two old men from *The Muppet Show?*

In a way, but there's not the cynicism, you know, not an urge to judge. It's more like this——Remember when I chaperoned your grade's field trip to Milledgeville? Before you went, before you read anything Flannery O'Connor had written, you'd thought she wasn't as worthy because she was southern and a woman, had the Catholic reputation and such, but the next summer, you took my copy of The Habit of Being *to that achievement camp at Duke. Do you remember what you said to me in a letter?*

I loved the book. It surprised me.

As did knowing I'd read it.

I know, and I'm sorry, really sorry, but what does it have to do with where you are now and being able to tell whether or not Ann loves me?

The connection is this, Wyatt, how she was capable of observing with a kind of critical distance, like someone on the outside looking in, or above Georgia looking down, but she was here.

In her yard, wasn't she, Mother?——like you and Dad, pigeons and peacocks.

And she knew things about this place, son, the same way I know things now, the same way I always knew what mothers are supposed to.

One of the reasons I've put off having children is I can't see myself being anything but ignorant and useless when I'm called on to know things about a daughter or, this is scary, a son. I couldn't look at a child and tell whether he's telling me the truth. So, what's the story on it, Mother? How'd you do it? How is it done?

Curiosity and desire, it's everything you need.

So self-centered people, they'd have difficulty doing it.

You'd think that, and you hear so much about movie stars paying too much attention to themselves to allow a child through, but it wouldn't be the case with you. I know it because I know you, know you'll rise to meet a daughter or son the instant the door's opened to the womb. Trust me, and also believe Ann loves you.

But why does she blame so much of what's wrong with us on me? She says I ignore her, but she's busier than I am, and I think I get so used to not seeing her, it's like not being married again, and when we're alone and I feel pressured to do the right thing or say something perfect to her, I'm thinking, she was gone, too.

Well, you're right, but if you insist on letting her know how right you are, you'll be sitting around alone and very self-satisfied somewhere.

But why can't she come to me? When did this become my responsibility?

When you were born a man, Wyatt, who didn't feel like a woman. Men are supposed to be heroes, and none of her education and successful career matters to her when she's with you. She's the girl, and you're the boy, and it isn't the girl who has her mother ride her to the florist for a corsage before the dances, and it certainly isn't the girl who stands outside the window, singing, because the person she loves is in her room crying.

Did Dad do those things for you?

Not the singing, and he never made me cry either. But my mother rode him to the florist before many dances and helped him pick out the freshest orchids for my corsages.

But does a flower matter that much? I mean, I feel like there was so much harm done while we were both working, not seeing each other much, distracted by money and how expensive everything but breathing was in northern California. And then, we borrowed from you and Dad, borrowed from her parents, and I look around at these other men my age out there with wives and families started, new cars, second houses, and I have absolutely no idea how they're all able to do it. So I don't see what difference it makes, giving Ann a picture frame, which I did, and a nice one, or giving her this ideal thing she had in mind that's still a mystery to me. The right present isn't going to change the fact that I don't know how to live my life.

She's told you it's the thought that counts.

Yes, but I could take off work for a month and make thinking about my wife's birthday present my job, and it wouldn't be good enough. I can't do things like Dad somehow manages, like giving her the ring.

It's his curiosity and desire that enable him to do it. You have to picture how she's feeling when she needs you, and you need to see your hand coming into view, correcting it, making things fine. You've allowed her to feel lonesome, son, and that's a fate a woman who married in good faith never intentionally calls for.

But I told you, she's let me feel that way, too.

And like I said, you can be right and be truly alone, or you can be the hero and give your wife a corsage.

If you were here to drive me downtown, I'd consider it.

What do you think I'm doing now?

Telling me my wife loves me.

Showing you how to choose orchids.

twenty-one

I'M GLAD YOU'RE HERE, ROSE. I KNEW YOU'D COME *down after Wyatt went up to bed.*

Where's the fire, Katy? I'm going to lay on top of the boy's scrambled pallet, and you tell me what it is that's the rush.

The florist we trade with, Freddy's, somebody's usually in there as early as seven, and I need you to ride Wyatt down there and help him find a nice orchid.

For you or his wife or just to have around the house? If it's for around the house, I'm ashamed to say it, but unless it's a philodendron, I'll have it killed in about a day and a half.

It's for Ann, and you need to not mention where you're taking him, if she's awake then.

Seeing a man and a dog sort of situation.

Yes.

Well, whatever an orchid's supposed to do, I hope it does

it, on account of they're barely civil. They're jumpy-making to be around. Did you find it to be the truth?

It was frustrating to know what was wrong and not feel able to do more than apply money to them to fix it.

Which never works.

Ephraim and I, Rose, we gave them five thousand dollars for Christmas one year, put it in an envelope with travel agency brochures about places we'd been to they'd shown some interest in. Now, if someone gave you that kind of money and suggested you spend it in Paris, Dublin, or Madrid, which would you do, take the trip or spend it on a better grade of television?

Damn, it must've been a hi-fi-stereo-television-combination.

Just an outsize TV with the tape machine things hidden in it, but tell me which you'd do. You'd take the trip, wouldn't you?

You know I would. I've been watching the same set since they came out with remotes. When that happened, I broke down and got a new one, but Katy, I'd be traveling by myself, not with a man I've lost my thrall to.

I know, and when they called and described how much of the bedroom wall was taken up now by the new TV, we knew things were about as bad with them as they could be.

They were probably in a good mood when they called, too, glad as hell to have an excuse not to speak or be spoken to.

She was on one phone to us, he was on the other, something they never do. You'd have thought they were calling about a baby being due.

But what I don't know is how he grew up here and had your husband and you and the way you are have so little influence, unless he was jealous of you being close.

He was, but when he was growing up, Rose, I didn't give any thought to it. Ephraim and I did what came naturally to us, and there was never any deliberate leaving Wyatt out of anything. We certainly never went off and left him, never turned him away from the bed when he was small and needed a nightmare or some small issue attended to.

But he would've known. He isn't a dummy.

It's interesting, you know, if his father and I'd fought constantly, he would've felt pushed to the side, been mad about the time and energy it took up, but Ephraim and I were there, reported for every little life activity. What he's missing is a way to use his good fortune.

And giving his wife an orchid is a starting place?

Yes, but he has to prove he thought about it and let her know it's urgent to him that he does something as large as giving her this small thing with an infinite amount of love inside it now. Ephraim'll see it and rest better tomorrow night. And it was thoughtful of Wyatt, but he has to continue. He'll need more than one better behavior on his record.

If you don't mind my saying, I think your husband's resting tonight because you're here, and not just because your son did it, but he seemed sincerely reviled by going back to Mr. Morgan's place.

Listen, Rose, and let me tell you this, and you can decide what to do with the news, though I trust you'll believe it. He's going to be with me, you see, sooner than people think his age and health qualify him to be.

Right away, as in tomorrow?

Not quite, but please, please take this in. I mean there'll come an instant, and when that instant's over, he'll be gone. He'll be on the other side of that one particular moment.

Well, what I can do, how can I help?

I want you to make him feel known, incredibly known until then.

I feel like I know him, I told him, like I know both of you.

Yes, but it's so much of it present, no history, and it's the thing most needed to speak directly to who he is.

Well, I'm up for the duration.

I know, but I'd rather my mother told you. She can explain—quite beautifully, actually—why he was dubious about going back to the funeral home this evening.

Is it ashes somewhere in the house I need to pull a seat up next to, or do I need to get my coat on and go over by her headstone at one of the cemeteries?

No, Rose, it's OK, nothing like that. You'll be a wealthy woman when all this is over, but no amount of money can compensate a woman for going to a cemetery by herself this deep of a January evening. All you need to do is look in the top of the chifforobe in your bedroom and read the letters from my mother I saved there. She wrote what amounted to books to me, much of it answers to questions I asked her about Ephraim, and she knew him well, you'll see. And then mix the history, Rose, with what you see and hear, what you know about human nature, and use everything you can to keep him filled until he gets here. You picked him up when he fell, knew he'd fall, told me, and now I'm telling you he can't feel empty.

He'll have to feel empty, Katy, at least not all the way whole, missing you, you understand, being his other half.

No, it's worse than that. Just consider it a minute, how we, neither one of us, used the other to complete us. When he sees the grave tomorrow, the hollow sensation that'll come then won't affect half of him, but the whole of him, Rose, because we lived in one another, you see, completely, and if he isn't offered enough substance, he'll believe there's nothing to him and consent to vanish.

And it won't be his time.

No, and I can't tell you when because it'd be human nature to dwell on it.

When what I need to be doing is giving him crackers.

Yes, from my mother's purse.

twenty-two

WHEN ROSE SQUEEZED WYATT HARD ON THE shoulder, whispering for him to get up and come with her without disturbing Ann, her night-smeared face bore a heinous resemblance to those of Baby Jane and Norma Rae Desmond, their features swirled around together on one of their rougher mornings. He didn't believe he had a choice, so after he'd dressed and washed his face, hoping the sound of water running in the guest bathroom meant she was doing the same, he met her in the hall and refused to take another step until she'd told him why.

"I'm riding you to the florist," she said, "so let's hit it."

"But we're not having flowers, just donations."

"I'm aware," she said, "but we're going to buy your wife a shoulder flower for her to have to wake up with, an orchid. I'll pick you out one and we'll get it, then I'd appreciate it if you wouldn't mind letting me run into my house a minute and get a housecoat and a few other things."

As many times as he asked her why, she'd say she couldn't tell him, but after the combat of buying the flower, his refusal to believe she hadn't been ordered to do this as a dying wish from the hospital bed, she apologized to the florist for the fit he'd thrown at the counter and more or less dragged him across the parking lot and shoved him into the car.

As they tore out, nothing was said until she jerked up in front of her white shotgun house, and though it was only half a mile from the florist, Wyatt had closed his eyes to try to force himself to sleep until everything was over. When he looked out over her bare yard to the bare porch, he said, "I have no idea where we are. This yours?"

"Yes," she said, "and what of it? You know what you are? A boy. Now come in and set there and be quiet for five minutes and let me throw some things in a soupcase. It might be too heavy for me to carry."

"Fine," he said, "not a problem."

"Hold the fort a minute," she said, "and let me tell you what the problem is. Now, you knew I was coming to get some personal items—what individuals generally pack in a soupcase—but it took me asking you, I mean, it absolutely did not occur to you to say, 'How about I go inside in case you may need help carrying your goddamn soupcase on account of I'm the man and you're the goddamn lady?'"

"And a goddamn one at that," he said.

"Tell it. And the other thing is, what I got hot about and continued overheating me is I tell you we're going to buy an orchid for your wife on the morning your mother's buried, one of somebody's red-letter days where you'd suspect some human emotion, and all you do is argue at me, thoroughly skipping over the fact that it's just a thoughtful gesture. That's all we were doing, making you up a thoughtful present to take to your wife to tell her you been thinking about her and how she might favor a flower or something such as that, and then she'd think you'd been thinking, and so on and so forth, and all I'm thinking is how goddamn glad I am not to be married. Now come help me get my mess. It defies me your mother and father were the ones to raise you. This is how people behave raised in the flippin orphan home."

He didn't want to sit down, as her house, he thought, smelled heavily of meat and cheese, and he didn't want to carry the smell around in his clothes, so he stood near the front door, which gave him a view through every room, back to where she was going around her sad, Spartan bedroom, picking up things and packing them in a cardboard soupcase. He wanted to know why she lived like this, why her home didn't have any stuff in it, and he was searching for an agreeable way to ask when she called out, "I'm ready for you to come tote this!"

Carrying it out, he waited for her to lock the door and then asked, "How long have you lived here?"

"Rented it when I was ten, nope, nine," she said. "Let's head on back to the house, got to get breakfast, get the pigeons fed, need you to run by the pet store later, see what they've got for delousing."

"For what?" he said.

"Delousing," she pronounced, throwing him against the door, swerving to make a U-turn, she said, "so the man that lives at the other end of the street doesn't come taking off after me. I paid the rent, but he believes I'm about to move and leave the house destroyed, owing more."

"I thought it looked neat," Wyatt said, thinking what a trick it'd be to make her house appear destroyed. "So, you grew up there?"

"Signed the lease when I was nine, parents had a wreck," she said, closing the subject.

"You signed something legal when you were nine?"

"I said the man was ruthless," she told him. "Candy from a baby, rent from a child, long as I paid it on time is all."

"Never married?"

"Worked," she said, "worked, watched television, worked, watched television. I understand it's more that goes on than that, but I could care less now and haven't, so I'm going to go to work fixing breakfast when we get to the house, and you're going to go make over the ring your father gave your wife, so think of something to say, and then you're going to pull the orchid out and give yourself credit when she says it matches the dress she's wearing to the cemetery today."

"You looked in the closet?"

"Yes," she said, "I did. I tend to stay a step ahead, which is advice I'd give any maritally-problemed man."

They were in the house when he believed she was calm enough to give him a civil answer to what had compelled her to sling him out on the trip, and while he sat on the sofa, looking at the orchid box in his hands, waiting for the nerve to interrupt her in the kitchen, she appeared with a stack of plates, muttering about having left the bacon on too high. She saw him glance at the casket before he stood and held his arms out for the dishes, saying, "My mother, she told me to get this orchid. I need to know how you knew."

Using the spatula he hadn't seen underneath the plates, she indicated the air above the casket, saying, "It's in the atmosphere is all. I didn't need somebody to tell me."

"What's in the atmosphere?" he said. "I mean, I'm not saying you'd be insane if you said you talked to my mother, so if she said something to you, you should tell me."

"I work here," she said, "and if the one that hired me was living, I wouldn't discuss what went on between us."

"But," he said, "she's not."

"All the more reason," she said, "to be decent and respect privacy or you may as well put somebody in a hellhole to have them mangled."

"I don't understand," he said. "Why can't you tell me?"

"Nothing matters," she said, "but what you did for your wife. Everything else anybody could need is, like I said, in the air, and if you want to know something, son, the ideas are out there."

After he left her to finish breakfast, she called the intensive care nurse Glenda and described how Ephraim had been on the verge of fainting, how little medicine he'd taken while I was hospitalized, and how pale he looked when she'd checked on him at dawn that morning. "Well, I was about to check the paper about the service," Glenda said, "so I'll see about him when I get to the church."

"Isn't a church," Rose said, "or the funeral home he's planned, just a few people at the cemetery, no more than a handful of others, or off to themselves as the two of them were, it could very well be just her family and us. She's in the living room now, in fact. Her son took and brought her back."

"You getting along OK with him?"

"He's a piece of work," she said, "the kind that's never carried a bucket. I can't tell what his job of work is."

"I know," Glenda said, "some kind of computer consulting, but that's all I can tell you because the time I asked him to explain, he all but said I wouldn't understand it. His wife seemed decent enough. They still together? Is she there?"

"Both," Rose said, "but barely."

They agreed to hustle Ephraim into the hospital if Glenda thought he required it, and as she shook his pills into her hand with the plan of putting them on his plate and refusing to put food there until they were taken, he opened the kitchen door and told her good morning. "There isn't a need to go get the other two," he said, nodding toward his son's room.

She said, "I wondered if he wouldn't go back to sleep."

"I can't tell if they're fighting or fooling around," he said, "but I'd wait either way."

"Then either way," she said, "they're living on love, so let's get you medicated and fed."

When he asked how her night had been, she regarded the two main truths of it, the conversation that had led to the florist and the letters that had led to long, ragged dreams of the ghoul snapping his mother's arm and to easier scenes of his mother-in-law installing Aunt Ruth into her new safe life, everything fresh and plumped, clean as a pen. She said, "It was fine, but listen, the messages are piling up on the telephone machine, and the sign I put on the doors, well, you can hear different individuals going away more or less vexed. They're going to see the paper this morning where it says it's just graveside services and know that's as good as saying everybody but immediate family should stay away."

"Let them stay vexed," he said, "and away. It isn't something we got mad at the world and decided. We planned it this way."

"You don't need to explain it to me," she said. "You need to chase a handful of pills with biscuits and gravy."

"I told Glenda to come, so I'd better bathe enough for her not to smell lard on my breath."

"It's only butter," she said. "Substance, Ephraim, bread and butter, something to weight you this morning, nourishment, you understand me, and if it's not enough, I'm a big-boned woman, Ephraim, so you take and grab me, you take and hold."

twenty-three

ANN AND WYATT HADN'T COME DOWNSTAIRS BECAUSE
they were twirled around one another in bed and
hadn't wanted to move. They hadn't had ten minutes of sheer
pleasure in as many years and they wouldn't risk disturbing
what felt as frail as the orchid Wyatt had pinned on Ann's
plain satin nightgown, ruining a patch of fabric, trying to get
it attached to her while he was kissing her throat. When Rose
walked by their door and heard them awake, she quickly
passed, thinking, Good for them, good for us all.

When Wyatt asked Ann to remind him to pay the minister, saying the fee was so little it'd be embarrassing to ask his
father, she said, "What did she believe in, exactly? It seems
like they would've arranged for a magistrate to, I suppose,
commit her to the ground if they thought they could get away
with it."

"I don't know," Wyatt said. "I almost want to say she believed in doing what felt good."

"She wasn't hedonistic," Ann said.

"But," he said, "what felt good to her, invariably, it was right, you know, ethical. I was a terrible bastard, used to describe her to people I knew wouldn't meet her like she was Gloria Steinem."

"The orchid's ethical."

"She said it'd be."

"I'd imagine she told you a great many things you ignored," Ann said, "but you ignored me before, when I asked you about going to Rose's house with her, when I asked how she lived. You know, if she's dirt-poor, Wyatt, we need to keep an eye on things, regardless of how your father feels."

Seeing the view through the house, he said, "No, I think she'll be fine. It was a fairly normal house for that area, where they used to have all the mills, and, well, she seems to work and go home and not do much of anything else."

"Well, maybe this is one of those times when something actually is what it appears. I so rarely see it at work, I suppose I naturally resist it."

"Did I tell you," he said, "my mother was in the news one time? I hadn't thought about it, but I remember seeing her picture in the paper, thinking there might be more to her than what appeared, and, you know, instead of asking her to tell me about it or praising her for what she'd done, I was mad at her for not showing that side of herself to me. Now I know it wasn't something she was hiding from me, just something, you know, ethical she did, and I bet my father still can't watch television and see somebody wearing a bulletproof vest without wanting to throttle me."

"What'd she do? Was she around when somebody was shot?"

"It was during integration," he said, "and hell was breaking loose every other day at school, so they hear about some riot being planned and give all the white teachers bulletproof vests, which made no sense because it was a white redneck group behind things, probably not with the idea of shooting a woman like my mother. Well, she understood, of course, and gave the vest they left in her office to the black science teacher who had the room next to hers, and open to the street, a wide row of windows that had already been broken out several times, glass flying in on her."

"So, Katy does this, thinking nothing of it."

"And it caused another kind of hell to break loose, arguments back and forth in the editorials, and then they interview her leaving school one day, asking, you know, why she'd done it, and she tells them, 'Because I wasn't the one with the target on me. Suppose I'd let her be killed? She has twin babies at home. Do they deserve to be without their mother because of some idiots, and no doubt illiterate? Ignorant people, shooting the school. Nobody deserves grief from one of these.' "

"You remembered it?"

"Yes," he said. "I thought, you know, I thought maybe I should, but the ring, Ann, looks good on you. Would you want another one if I gave it to you after a baby was born?"

"Yes," she said, "I think maybe I would."

twenty~four

WALKING CLOSE BESIDE ROSE ACROSS THE GRAY cemetery lawn, toward Mr. Morgan's green tent and the two young men who'd had the decency to wait for him to be taken out of the back door of the house before they went in the front door to take me away, Ephraim said, "I decided what you are, set here to get me to the other side of this. You're not a stranger, just strange, and I believe that comes as a compliment for you."

"I worked for a woman one time," she said, "that had all the state mottoes painted on eggs she blew, you know, like Easter, and she decorated them around with the main crop or the state's claim to fame, and I'll give you a hundred thousand dollars if you can guess which one I dropped dusting and broke."

"North Carolina," he told her, then recited the state motto, " 'To be rather than to seem,' but I'll take a dollar. I don't suppose you could put together a hundred."

"You want to say, 'Unless it came from me,' but we could stop by the bank on the way back if you care for the hundred."

My son, the young man who looked incredibly like my husband, was waiting by the tent, and they were too close for Rose to tell Ephraim anything other than he should ask his son when he said he was stupefied to think she was worth that figure of money and was curious to know where it'd come from. Ann and Wyatt were meeting Glenda in a cleared place, walking together now and asking themselves why the sight of Rose there wasn't jarring, why her presence wasn't large, and why she was so quiet-looking, not a sound coming off her hair or her clothes.

When Wyatt thanked Glenda for being there, she said, "It's an honor, you know, because your parents didn't allow many people in, and I felt, well, privileged to see something other people don't see. I used to think Ephraim and Katy made the impression they did because of their age, like they'd come out of another century, but actually I think what they had was, you know, timeless."

Wyatt said, "I used to think I was the only one to see it."

"People at the hospital," she said, "noticed and couldn't figure it out. More than one said they were like movie stars, carrying whatever it is they have around them. However, Dr. Woodward treated them like ordinary people, maybe because he thinks he's all that exists. If he could see who they were, it'd change him, give him what he needs."

When they were all gathered, Ephraim handed the minister a paper, and Rose, brushing back her hair, leaned toward Glenda and whispered, "Remind me to ask you about borrowing something hospital-strength that's good to delouse."

The winter light was a raw white, and as it reflected off the bronze coffin into Glenda's eyes, she couldn't make out more than a sheen of Madame C. J. Walker's spray wax, a product for black hair Rose favored, and she decided that if shoals of lice escaped her hair, they'd have to skate over the ice down her head and the ice on the ground, assuming they'd drop and not—she shivered—crawl onto someone else. Wyatt reached over and lifted up the collar around the back of Glenda's coat, saying, "Colder than it was, colder," and then he lifted up Ann's hand with his other, showing his father how the ring looked in the light, turning her hand. Ephraim recognized, remembered, and said aloud, realizing it, but not caring he was being heard to confess, "I stay evermore grateful to your daddy for raising you so well, so well-cared for, Katy. I wish I'd shown him your hands to let him know how I kept you, my home, my Katy, kept very, very well."

Rose said, "Oh, Ephraim, he knew. He knew already, when he bought the suits of clothes for you."

Wyatt said, "He had to"; and Ann said, "Fathers do," as Glenda looked at the minister, telling him to agree. Afraid he'd ramble and irritate them, Wyatt caught him just before he spoke and said, "It'd probably be better if I went ahead and read what's on the paper, a poem Mother liked, I think."

Ephraim said, "No, son, it's a letter her mother sent, last one before she died."

Wyatt took the letter, unfolded it, and read—

Dear Katy,

Odd to write to you when you're in the house and I could stomp a coded message to you or tell you in person, as smart as you are about answering the fetching-bell Ephraim installed for me. He said he stole it when he was in the hospital, and I can't tell if he actually did it, but if he did and would be prone to another crime, could you ask him to crawl up into the window and take the bed jacket they wouldn't sell me when we were downtown the other day, when they behaved like it'd be a tragedy to change the mannequin's outfit in the middle of the season.

I told them it'd be yellowed and worthless by winter, and you saw the stubbornness, so, to my mind, not only were they not going to profit from the bed jacket, they may actually deserve to find it gone. I wish I felt like a walk that far today, but my usual turn down the hall this evening may be it for now.

I have to write you, Katy, because I like to, and also to warn you against Our Town. I'd never watched it for fear it was sappy, and I avoided reading it because it sounded depressing, but let me tell you, if the actors are reading the words as they were written exactly, it rattles my belief in what you and your father have done for a living, handing out alleged literature to children. If I had a guarantee a plague was going to wipe Our Town out shortly, I could endure another few minutes, just to have something besides my stomach to lay this dull pain to.

I cut the damn thing off, Katy, as life is too short, always in general, as a guiding rule, but short now in a measured way, like the small steps your Aunt Ruth began to take toward the end, slowly down the hall of her lovely house, step by step, nodding after each one, approving the accomplishment. Wyatt walked that way when you had him here the other morning, in his own world, deliberating some great notion of an imagined pleasure, no doubt splendid and real as life to him. And too, my girl, I've seen you and Ephraim live in your own world and move forward with it safe around you, holding it around, as you, your father, and I did when we moved out to the end of the road you found love on and brought him home.

I'm afraid sometimes that the way you learned to be was too isolated, and you'd miss the comforts some find in a larger company, but I did what I knew, and to be raised another way, you would've needed to be born to other parents. Maybe I should stomp and ask you if I did all right, but you told me yesterday and the day before, and you and Ephraim, when you brought Wyatt in this morning and put him there to color his pictures at the foot of my bed, and you combed my hair and pulled your mouth all open and had me look inside to divine the matter with your tooth, you told me, tell me habitually.

Always tell them, Katy, keep it your life's work to let them know they're adored and worshipped down to their feet and beyond, my girl, down past time and words, all meaning, spread out into everything that has existed and is waiting to be here, let them know your love—I believe that's all there is, oh, and I forgot to say you do such a pretty job bleaching Wyatt's shoes.

I hear you. I hear your voice, and leaving you for now, until I'm able to rise and take my slow walk to your room, I will be filled with love, all love for you,

Your mother

Ephraim knew better than lure himself with the temptation of letting the ground take me, but did it willfully anyway, so filled with anger over the lost love and wreckage, everything my mother'd said now firmly shot straight to hell, that when Rose offered him the big bone of her arm, he said, "I'll be goddamned before I take it."

Letting him stay behind, the four of them walked to the cars, reluctant to talk about anything beyond Rose's need to get rid of bird and not head lice. Glenda finally said, "I'm sorry to say it, but he doesn't look well. He hasn't looked well for weeks. I would've had him admitted the day Katy died, but he wouldn't have stayed. He's trying, and he'll tell you otherwise, but he's giving out."

"Not giving up," Rose said. "Respectable. She said it wouldn't be long, though."

"My mother?" Wyatt asked.

"She and Rose," Glenda said, "spent a long time together right after they met."

Ann said, "And Wyatt, I'd imagine your mother told Rose a great many things she didn't ignore."

"She did," Rose said, "but sometimes a thing isn't more

than what it looks like to you, being, seeming, so it isn't a mystery why an eighty-year-old man with the stress of a sick and then passed-away wife would seem to be slipping, on account of the man earned the right to and probably is."

Closing herself in the backseat of Ephraim's car, she waited, thinking, "Goddamn if I didn't like to of almost had a thing. How is it other people get something to do and somewhere to be in between work and the television set? If that's all there's ever going to be to this, then open the ground up and vanish me in. He can be kept well. Do what she said do and keep him whole, well."

Wyatt, simply put, realized he should be ashamed for leaving his father out there, so went back to where Ephraim had sat on one of the few chairs under the tent, noticing that his lips looked wafer-thin and blue, saying, "This is enough, let's get you into the heat."

"No," Ephraim said, "let's speed it."

Wyatt said, "But you can't sit here into perpetuity, Dad. The reality is, in a few minutes you'll need to leave, and other than that, I don't know what to say except I'm sorry you have to go through it. I can't let you stay in this cold, though, it's bitter."

"It's that," he said. "As much as she did for the goddamn universe, you'd think they could've warmed the ground for her. And you were right, son, she's not here, I see it, I am full of understanding, she isn't here."

"You told me to remember her, made it sound evil not to."

"I'd prefer a coma to remembering."

"But the women, they were just talking about how well you were doing."

"Maybe I was, or I wasn't, but it doesn't matter. I've only got now and going forward, and things, I'm telling you, have ceased to be real."

"Then let's go home, and see if anything's better."

By the time they reached the cars, Wyatt was carrying Ephraim in his arms, legs dangling like a tall boy's, and when he took his father out of the car and then up the steps to the house, Ephraim said, "You heard it snap. They broke her, and I need to be here now, with everything else gone. Put a record on or let's just have Katy talk."

"She will," Wyatt said, taking him through the door, suddenly amazed at how light the burden had been, "and I mean it, Dad, I'm telling you the absolute truth, just listen and before you know what's happened, you'll realize Mother's been talking to you."

twenty-five

A YEAR LATER, ROSE EXPLAINED HER HEALTH MAIN-
tenance routine for the pigeons to the woman she'd
met at the luncheonette the first time she had a leisured meal,
which she regarded as one not eaten sitting in front of her
television set or standing by a conveyor belt or in a kitchen she
was cleaning. She outlined the benefits of the hospital-strength
eyedrops, disinfectants, and delousing agents, and when the
woman asked if she was planning to stay in the Doyals' house,
she said, "I feel I'm meant to, and I can rest there, so, yes, and
the thing of it is, what's always going to strike me is it took a
handful of days to let me see I could live the life I wanted to
be living, as plain an issue as that sounds."

"Well, who were you living it for beforehand, Rose?" the
woman asked.

"Oh, hell," Rose said. "I don't even know that I've ever

known that. Maybe I thought if I worked hard enough, it'd eventually bring some peace of mind back."

"You look good," the woman said, "rested in the face, so peace of mind, I suppose, didn't get to you too late."

"Hold the fort and oh hell again," Rose called out across the table. "It wasn't ever like I was broke, I had a roll ready-banked for retirement or a bad paralysis, and had I been able to stop working a minute and let go of some of it, I could've gotten over to the Ritz-Carlton in Atlanta, where they fairly sell it."

The only problem Rose had with being out and about, meeting new people, was that none of them were what she thought of as being especially bright; and except on days when she ate in the cafeteria with Glenda, she found herself droning on to explain things when her mind had long since clicked on to the next topic. She already had her mouth set to say she'd fallen in thrall with subtitled movies, nothing she'd anticipated, the kind of thing she'd felt on the lower rung of until she discovered all the channels that came with the new television Wyatt and Ann had sent on her birthday. But the woman wanted to be told, "What do they sell at the Ritz-Carlton? I mean, when you go stay, is it when they're running a peace of mind special, like at this Hilton I used to work at where they gave you shopping coupons and a bottle of champagne, manicures and Elton John tickets? He moved here, you know. I heard it was hard to get on with him to clean. He wants you English."

"I don't know from a Hilton," Rose said, "and no offense, but from the outside, they look a little dirty, and if Elton John calls for English help, he's got an eye for smart, take it from me, and what the hell was it you asked me, oh, the peace of mind thing."

The woman said, "I have to live through you on it or I wouldn't have a flippin life."

"Don't say that," Rose told her, "and bite your lip if you're on the verge of telling it. Tell it enough and watch it be real. I said all I did was work for so long that damned if it didn't become all I did, didn't know what else to say when somebody asked me to say in so many words who I was. I'd more or less say 'worker,' like a communist."

"They make those women wear gray clothes," the woman said, "and everything's like public television, you know, nothing selling on the commercials."

"No Hiltons, probably no Howard Johnsons," Rose said, deciding not to tell her friend nothing operated in the black-and-white she was imagining life behind the Iron Curtain playing in, as she wasn't confident enough to put things into words quite yet, only recently comfortable with the decisions she'd made concerning the possibility of sudden bursts of grace and explosions of plenty inside barren places. And although reading my mother's letters had become a daily habit, she wasn't nonchalant about the instruction she found there, believing it'd be a violation to tell the woman that life is being nourished, is being sheerly poured on everywhere and at all times, keeping even un-American lifestyles cycling.

"I can't imagine," the woman said, "but I can't imagine the peace of mind special at the Ritz either unless you tell me."

Saying she'd rather narrate walking, they took the route along a downtown street where Rose was now able to drop in to some of the smaller ladies' places and ask about the cut she noticed to be similar in the same line of clothes or try on something universally tasteful without feeling some physical symptoms of stroke. She wasn't certain whether there'd ever come a time when she allowed the chattering Vietnamese ladies to manicure her ridged nails, but she was working toward believing they'd seen everything before, particularly given where they were from. These women knew about starvation and starch.

When they were beside the window of the drugstore where she'd bought her hair products since puberty, when everything, she often thought, took and popped out big, she pointed to her spray wax displayed and said, "At the Ritz-Carlton, when I went to the salon to get my hair fixed on account of I wanted to go to the mall movies that evening, the lady asked me what I generally used on my head, and I didn't know what to tell her and couldn't say nothing so I told the truth and said Suave Egg shampoo and Madame Walker's as the fixative. She was young, so I expected her to choke laughing, not be able to respect, but she was very nice to me— offered, I mean, to go out and get the things, I mean, in a bag, and bring them back into the Ritz-Carlton salon and use them on my head."

The woman said, "Well, did she, Rose? Tell me, and then tell me the rest of it. I'm interested."

"I told her to use what she usually did," Rose said, "and said if I enjoyed it, I'd buy some to take home for the house. Then, while I was sitting there waiting for the color stripper to set, which was going to be a tedious while, I told her, on account of Rome wasn't built in a day and neither was this redhead, and like she could read my mind that I'd love nothing more than to take a knockout pill to get through sitting still so long, she took and ran a vibration instrument over my shoulder muscles, up on my neck to where my teeth fairly buzzed, and when I woke up, I swear to you, I was completely done. She'd leaned me back and more or less made me look like a flippin million dollars entirely all in my sleep."

"You probably tip somebody that does that."

"Hell, yes," Rose said, "and when you leave the salon, it keeps coming at you, more than you can take at once, until you need to rest from resting. And I know they're paid very well to be accommodating to everybody, but they have a way of making you believe they'd love nothing better than to get out of their beds in the middle of the night and run around to hither and yon, like it's a goddamn honor going and doing for you. And the peace of mind they offer there, well, what you find out is you're the one to bring it, and they simply serve it to you or use it on you, the way I was welcome to bring my brand of shampoo and spray wax in with me. Except for the bed, there isn't anything there you couldn't do for yourself at home, I mean, if you had a grocery store that sold the right food and the cooking network on."

The woman said, "But it'd be bound to be nothing that felt as good."

"Tell it!" Rose shouted. "And it's peace of mind and human satisfaction that comes on when you realize you're able to buy the order of rest they're selling because you're one of these that worked and loved like it was the absolute and our all."

twenty-six

Dear Wyatt,

Just a note to say I'm writing you a letter. I will tell you why later.

As Glenda told you and Ann when you left for California, it was either I stay for a duration in the hospital with her or stay for timeabouts unknown at home with Rose. I understand you were upset because I wouldn't allow you and her to vary my choice even though you behaved about it. You have no way of knowing what I'm about to tell you unless I'd told you, but I wasn't any better capable of turning around my father once he hit the road toward something than you are with me, me being under eight back then and trying to keep him from drinking, migrant Puerto Rican women, taking beatings for counting cards, and you name it until a light went off and told me neither I nor nothing could bring him back from running away. You needed to have that on the first page.

Rose has not left me alone a minute. Glenda comes after her shift and spells her for a few hours. You were right about the insurance company not consenting to pay for machines the doctor ordered and sent and since I'd rather be killed by a weak heart than a strong band of thieves, I said to hell with it and paid. From what I understand, the damage to muscle and tissue means there isn't enough time left to be out too much, but you still need to study the final bill because what they overcharge spells less for your family and Rose and the group Katy liked to give book money to.

You sounded set on ready to come, and I appreciate it, and whenever you come is fine, but it isn't necessary. If Rose hadn't taken things in hand and made me feel more settled than I was the day of the funeral, I'd be saying to come right on just to see if you would. One day is like the other, but it's fine. I feel like I'm in a waiting room where they distract you away from the slow-passing time with a buffet, a run of good movies on the television set, and a comfortable nap pallet.

You made it sound like you believed you need to rush here to keep me from swallowing a poison pill or escaping down to the railroad tracks to end everything with a train. Ann's smart on facts of human nature and has met many individuals with a despairing case of the blues, and she was right to diagnose me with a new peace of mind when we three spoke the other evening, but you need to stop trying to lay it to a decision I've made to take my life on account of I haven't. Which is not to say I wouldn't mind waking up in a world where Katy is in the morning. I've made that plain, but I need you to be patient a minute and listen through me being completely honest with you so no one's left with any questions.

After you left and took the worry of you walking in a room and finding me, Rose said I had the look of somebody ready to do something and took everything I could use and would not allow me in the toilet with the door closed. Then two things happened that made me take and get up out of the hell I was in and go on to where the waiting would be satisfactory.

The first was Ann telling me about the blood testing, and even though your child is only three weeks old, I can tell you in no time he'll be thirteen and then thirty, and if I've stayed so ashamed of your grandfather leaving out on my mother and me that it took to now to say more than a word about it, I hated to think I wouldn't live for your girl or boy because you couldn't speak of what his grandfather did to himself, and memories of Katy that're wrapped around in mine would naturally be set in more of a corner in your mind. I don't mean you'll be dilating on what a great fellow I was, but if you need to use a way we clanged on a matter to explain something to a son, it means a great deal to me to know I'd be there available.

So it was more or less the future talking to me, and then the second matter had to do with the past, with the letters Rose brought in here and began reading to me. She began bringing in shoeboxes full of postcards, telegrams, and the long letters Katy got from her mother continuously whether they had five thousand miles between them or none. Son, it was like she was taking everything Katy's mother had ever said to Katy out of the box and putting it in me. I didn't feel as empty and then I started feeling the way you do after too much Thanksgiving. Rose won't say how many boxes are left, though we just passed you being born where she answers your mother on how to ignore my housekeeping.

If I don't sound exactly like me, know I'm going through Rose, so what you hear in your mind's ear is more us mixed. I forgot to say it was something to hear Katy's mother again, and this is not in my writing because I'm dictating to Rose. Who just said to say you might hear Katy, too, on account of her way of talking favored her mother's and we'd read four of the letters. She also said to tell you the reason was to let me see what that's like and it's the only time it happens.

She also says she thinks you had the right idea to move to Florida in plenty of time for the birth because it will spare the baby growing up with people thinking he or she is irresponsible because of being born in California and says if you get the smaller house you said you were set on, if you plan not to have room for the outsize television set, she wishes you'd have the moving men drop it off here on their way through Georgia.

I know you got upset after we talked about the baby, but I have every faith in you as a father. You can't continuously look back and wish you hadn't made certain decisions or dwell on what you called your mother and me bailing you out when you earn a good wage and all that sort of matter. What I heard, son, is a man who wants to know he's in control of his life before he brings a human being into the world to raise. I'm not going to lie and say I admire every decision either one of us made, but I admire the man you've become, which is one who knows the kind of father and husband and worker he needs and wants to be and sets himself in that direction with all the strength in him.

Don't worry that people might look down on what you do to accomplish what you called simplifying as not being up to the par of their high style of living. For one, it's your business and they don't take care of your family. And Wyatt, you don't want people around your family anyway that don't wish you well, and anybody that sees you put your values to a strong purpose will say what a good man you are to be the safe place a woman and child need.

You don't need to prove honor to me, though, by following through on every future plan you have, and several sound too drastic. If I were you,

I'd go on to Florida and find the smaller house with less upkeep near Ann's parents and make a schedule to retire your high-interest debt. That order of plan makes sense, but I wouldn't get rid of the Mercedes on account of it's paid for and you won't get the value, and I haven't had better than an Impala but if I could get up and go somewhere, I'd buy a nice automobile to ride around in these days. It'll make you feel good. I can't estimate how much you can expect directly, but I believe your idea to not touch it for a year or until you feel like you've met your mark is wise. You said you could buy your company's insurance and Rose said any premium you have to pay for maternity is fine because she's known new parents to be eaten alive. The last practical issue is she's going to continue staying here. She gave the proper notice to her landlord who I tried to talk to on the telephone and is a bastard. If he gives her any kind of trouble, she says to tell you she won't need it but I'm asking you to step in front of him for her.

You wouldn't think the first letter a person wrote since 1946 would tire me like this, especially since I'm only talking it out, but there are just a couple things more I want to sum up and explain. I want you to remember to give your wife the chance to take care of you, and if you get where you don't know what she needs right then, it'll come to you if you feel in her shoes. You're the only one who can organize it to where, in the end, satisfactions are piled so high that you can't see the puny stack of disappointments you accumulated for the tall shadow of pleasures. We're both doing fine, son, you with the woman you love and a child on the way, and me soon to be with mine. Everything will be fine.

I love you, son,
Your father

Through to the
Other Side of Air

EPHRAIM TOLD HIMSELF HE WAS OWED A TRIP OUT-
side, and on the last day of January, he took advantage of a late afternoon sliver of time between Rose's departure and Glenda's arrival to go. Rose had trusted him, but he'd be back in bed in a few minutes, particularly since he couldn't lift his coat over his shoulders and was wearing only his robe and pajamas in the raw cold and damp.

He wanted to walk to the edge of the field and visit the pigeons, and as he reached the middle of the yard, the first streak of pain ripped across his chest and dug in, as though driven by main strength to rout around, cutting until his flesh had been hacked away from his bones. A maniac seemed to have set upon him, and now he was reaching down into this burning, yawing, and rent place and ripping his shoulder from his body in one swift, brutish jerk. He fell and lay on his side just as a flame began scorching the surface of the pain, destroying it finally and leaving him bewildered to think he'd be attacked so furiously in his own yard. He turned his head and vomited scrambled eggs, but he didn't remember having eaten eggs since my mother's poached ones, so he decided his heart had exploded into pieces that had come up into his mouth.

When he could still see, he regarded his location, the field and trees across the wide span of grass, the pens full of healthy birds to one side, the town to the other. Then the lights began going down gradually, saving him at least from sudden alarm, lowered by my mother and his from where they watched against intruders from the porch as he began falling out into the singular purpose of love, everywhere now where everything else had been. The ease was instant and enduring, and as he folded into the heart of our love, he felt himself taken into familiar arms, and we said, Here now, then, always loved you, here now with me, in and around us, always loved you and will.

The
Other
Side
of Air

JEANNE BRASELTON

A READER'S GUIDE

Afterword

by KAYE GIBBONS

I want to tell you a story about a woman who called me early one morning, convinced that I was her only means of escape from a world of bills and babies. I want to tell you about her because I can still hear Jeanne howling with laughter when I called that afternoon and described the encounter. She would often goad me into retelling the story, laughing out loud all over again, as though hearing it for the first time. The story also helps to explain who Jeanne Braselton was and who she was not, and as odd as it sounds, I wanted to get it down on paper, inside the covers of her book, so she would have it with her, a sort of last-minute gift of memory for a long, long journey. Whoever said "You can't take it with you" hadn't traveled with Jeanne. Of all the things I hope she has now— peace of mind, of body, and of spirit—I also hope she has her enormous red suitcase by her side and that it is overflowing with memories, with stories she read, heard, told, and loved.

I need to tell another story first, one that will show that unless a writer is startled by an excellent and rigorous mind and a determined attitude, as I was with Jeanne Braselton, there is very little a reader can do that will surprise us. From outright demands and borderline threats to offers of free vacation rentals, office furniture, babysitting, and casseroles, though never the obvious bribes of sex or money—I hear it all. A writer becomes accustomed to the reader who stands in line at signings, waiting for the opportunity to thrust forward a manuscript or to propose some brilliant and original idea that the writer can simply type up and cause to be published by a major concern and marketed to the masses, making both the thinker-upper and the typer-upper outrageously rich and famous. It happens so often, in fact, that I have developed a theory about it that allows me to spot these readers in line. They are never holding a newly purchased book, and they are generally wearing a hat.

Jeanne happened to be with me when this first story unfolded. She was standing behind my chair at a signing when a man wearing a cowboy hat came at me with a plan rather than a manuscript. As he was about to disclose the thesis of "our" novel, he intimated a bothersome concern over whether he should wear socks during his inevitable interview on the *Today Show*. Jeanne began poking my shoulder, hard, whispering, "Tell him to lose the hat." He seemed to have rehearsed his televised debut countless times and appeared to be stricken by anxiety, on the verge of weeping or grabbing me from across the table, generally overwhelmed by the task of creating the right impression when being questioned about a novel that I imagined to be, and by now hoped would stay, locked in somewhere underneath his Stetson.

Jeanne continued to whisper retorts and poke. She had met me there in Atlanta after having nursed her husband, Al Braselton, through a particularly arduous recovery from one of his intermittent and increasingly dangerous battles with heart disease. Her first novel, *A False Sense of Well Being*, was about to be published. Both Jeanne and this man were waiting for an answer, as were the people waiting behind him, so I told him that Russell Crowe or George Clooney could go sockless on national television with aplomb, but I really couldn't say what he should do about his own feet, as I had not been on the *Today Show* and thus was ignorant of this particular rule of etiquette. Appalled, he took his original idea over to Garrison Keillor's line. After I was through signing, Jeanne lifted her skirt well over her knees and asked, "You think Katie'd like me better if I shaved these legs?" I told her I didn't know about Katie Couric, but I certainly would, as would a dozen transfixed onlookers. As we walked out of the room, laughing, we saw the nervous man, still in line, still awaiting his pain-free literary deliverance.

Some people skip the personal meeting altogether and choose to mail in their efforts or phone in their ideas. The woman who so intrigued and delighted Jeanne phoned me in the winter of 2001 at 7:30 in the morning and said she could make both of us outrageously rich and famous. She sounded serious, very serious. There was something almost holy about the sound of her desperation. As I listened, I considered asking her to hang on while I sorted out how to conference Jeanne in on the line, but as I was clueless about how to actually do this and didn't want to risk losing her, I decided to take notes.

She described herself as twenty-three, the mother of four, with another one on the way, the victim of all five of their various fathers, some jailed, some not, without rent that month, and, she said, "worn out, played out, and about to be put out of my unit if I don't find something quick." Later, Jeanne would ask, as I wanted to, why she had been able to find an unlisted phone number instead of gainful employment, but I could not ask—not with the nightmarish clatter and wails of her small children rising up in the background. So I asked what I could do for her. Her scheme was ingenious. I could ghostwrite the story of how she had gotten into her current predicament, send it to my agent, and so forth. She would, she said, "talk it out to you on the phone, either right now or later today, and then you can sell it for, I don't know, a half a million, and then you'd get some, and I'd get some. And do you think they could get it to me next week?"

I suspected that it would be a matter of minutes before I was called a bitch (a dead-on prediction). As I stood in my kitchen, my three teenage daughters set up their regular, almost elegantly orchestrated clothing brawl. The thirty-pound cat was on the stove, eating instant grits, and could not be heaved off. I had not slept for fear of being sued by the man who had, just the day before, knocked his front teeth out while jackhammering up our living room, which had sunk and pulled away from the rest of the house. Later that day, Jeanne would shout, "Kaye, you were talking to the woman on a damn slope! And you were broker than she was! I'd have hung up!"

But Jeanne wouldn't have hung up. She would've continued to listen, and she would've been generous beyond her means. When the young woman told her that it would take only an hour or two to get her "up to speed," she would've found all the time in the world. But she would have been stunned, as I was, if she had told the woman that she was late taking children to school, that she needed to do this another time, only to hear a tirade of invective and accusation. When the woman screamed, demanding that I tell her what the hell I expected her to do, I told her that I'd find some birth control, a babysitter, and a job, in that order. I can still hear Jeanne asking me, "At what point did she call you a bitch?" I wasn't sure, but my notes said it was about the same time the cat jumped into a sink full of dirty dishes.

As Jeanne and I talked about this woman's quest, two themes were predominant, both important to her outlook on life and literature. That I was engaged in something literary, as offbeat an enterprise as it was that morning, in the middle of so much domesticity, appealed to her. She loved Flannery O'Connor's collection of letters, *A Habit of Being,* and would often compare my five cats to O'Connor's peacocks. She was in favor of, in immutable love with, the idea that a woman could create a work of value, or try to, surrounded by the needs of a home and the needs of children. She celebrated the fact that a woman could get up from her writing and run loads of laundry between chapters, that a woman could sit in a middle school auditorium one night and on a university stage the next. It was the interweaving of authentic life and authentic art that Jeanne treasured.

One night, well after midnight, she called as I was cleaning out the freezer. I had wanted to keep writing but had exploded a Diet Coke while attempting to quick-chill it, and I did not want my daughters to find that I had done this yet again. When Jeanne asked what I was doing, I told her that I was wiping out the freezer with Clorox and thinking about how Umberto Eco was probably, at that moment, reclining on a divan somewhere on the Left Bank, grooving on having been named Umberto. She said, "But can Umberto Eco eat off the floors under his beds? I don't think so. Go back to work, honey."

So it was this confluence, as Eudora Welty would have called it, of life and art that gave Jeanne such hope that women who chose a literary life would be able to manage, to produce a strong and vibrant legacy of fiction. She thought in large, broad strokes like that. She could take the small, quotidian act of cleaning out one's freezer while an unfinished novel rested in the other room and find similarities in her vast, deep knowledge of literary history and conclude that combining life and art was a blessing for women writers rather than our plight. Sometimes we would make plans to talk after my girls had gone to bed, and one of us would have to postpone it, either because her husband needed her or I had homework to check. She would say, "Al's not feeling well, Kaye. We'll have to be geniuses together later."

Once real life was taken care of, our conversations were often about what we were reading. My list was usually embarrassingly strange, but she understood and could make phenomenal suggestions. Sometimes a strange assortment of books about whatever strange subject was dominating my reading would appear on my doorstep. She hunted down and had sent to me boxes of books on the treatment of female hysteria, on Civil War battlefield medicine. She put me on hold while she called a priest and asked him to explain the meaning of certain morning and evening prayers.

Coincidentally, long before we met, we had both read *The Great Gatsby* over the course of a single summer day, that time of year chosen because this is when Jay Gatsby is shot as he floats in his beautiful pool. Jeanne knew that novel in such an intimate way, as she did every word Eudora Welty and Walker Percy ever wrote. Her reading selections were catholic and eclectic—she could speak with great enthusiasm about a passage from *The Portrait of a Lady* and then recite some strange tidbit from the current *National Enquirer* or the *Weekly World News.* She was in love with language, and it didn't matter where the language appeared, as long as it was pure, accurate, and without the cynicism and pretense that she decried in life and literature.

It was not uncommon for her to send along odd obituaries or wedding announcements from local newspapers, with particularly outstanding details underlined. Jeanne's first training as a writer was in the society department of a newspaper in north Georgia. I can hear her right at this moment, describing the day a mother of the bride reached into her purse and brought out a pistol, which she held on Jeanne until Jeanne agreed to fix certain elements of her daughter's "write-up." And Jeanne would say, "They had my corner of the newsroom furnished in cheap French provincial furniture, the kind you get from Sears, and I rewrote that announcement with a gun pointed at me, and it was loaded, Kaye. The damn woman had her finger on the trigger."

Jeanne and her husband, Al, had a knack for reading and absorbing what they read while watching television, something I still consider a feat. And they carried on a running conversation, a lifelong conversation, as they sat there and read aloud to one another. It was a marvelous thing to witness. When we brought Al home from the hospital, just after Jeanne had published *A False Sense of Well*

Being, he settled into his favorite chair and, weakly but with heart-breaking conviction and commitment, said, "I'm so proud of Jeanne I can hardly stand it." I had never been in the presence of such tenderness and doubt I ever will be again.

She and Al had no children of their own, but Jeanne communicated with my daughters with great aplomb, and she talked to them as though they were fully grown, which they appreciated. They also appreciated her generosity. When I refused to put televisions and video players in their rooms, they reported this atrocity to Jeanne during one of her long, lovely sojourns at our house. I can see her with them by the tall windows in our loft, saying, "Your mama won't get you what? Everybody ought to have a damn television in the bedroom." Within a week after she left, a man arrived with a great deal of audiovisual equipment purchased by Jeanne. As he hooked it all up, I called her. She was already laughing when she picked up the phone.

Jeanne, more than any other person I have known, understood that a modern woman who is writing to earn her living, particularly in the South, must be capable of an abiding faith in the ordinary and the sublime, that she cannot choose one over the other if both her heart and her mind are to thrive. Jeanne trusted that a woman could haul a load of children to the movies, take her husband to the doctor, get a manicure, and come home from all her dailyness, sit down in front of a blank sheet of paper, and express the highest aspirations of mankind. She believed that the lot of us, we washers of dishes and folders of laundry, could approach what Balzac and Zola had accomplished in what we perceived to be their more rarefied environments. She saw nothing foolish or unreasonable in our efforts, and she had little patience for people who thought that our subjects were somehow of less value than those selected by Philip Roth or John Updike—she would point out that their work is also grounded in the life of a home, in what the characters were taught, and in their memories, and the fact that their locales were northern did not make their work any stronger or more enduring, for we all write from the same place. She could swiftly list enough details of place, of home, of a certain connectedness to one time and one place in *Madame Bovary* to convince any skeptic that this was as regional a tale as had ever been told. And then she would describe what made the novel take the leap into the sphere of classic literature, how the emotions and concerns, the fears and hopes of Charles and Emma are ours, that we know them, and they are us. She once told me that Flaubert "covered his ass well" by paying such careful attention to both the particular habits and customs of the setting and these universal themes.

The other theme that comes to mind when I think of Jeanne's reaction to the early-morning call has to do with her attitude toward what she and I called intellectual responsibility. The woman on the phone, the cowboy in line, weren't quite reconciled to the amount of hard labor and concentration, the sheer pain, required to write any book of value, especially one that would impress the national media and hordes of readers. Jeanne used to say, "Never trust a writer until she's had a baby or worn paper shoes," and while I'm sure that the woman caller and the cowboy qualified on one front or the other, their approach to writing was that of a hobbyist. And this is fine, Jeanne would say, if that's what you want to do. Then she would roll her big eyes. Writing requires intellectual stamina and a punishing bent toward self-criticism, almost an ease with examining what has been written and finding it worthless. Then the writer must do whatever best enables him to start over, to repeat this horrifying process until there is a book, or a chapter, or even a line that makes him feel as if it can be shown to another person, who will either find it worthy or not. The high and low points of this process are inherently treacherous and not to be underestimated in their ability to wound or exhilarate the person who is setting the purest element of what makes him human, his language, up for public scrutiny.

On the other side of all the labor is the company of other people who have endured the same ordeal, who speak that same language. In the South, we have a sort of historic kinship among ourselves, which probably comes from the fact that every writer here has an active and urgent gratitude for the amazing opportunities we have had as writers. Jeanne knew our history. She could tell you that after the Civil War there was an unabashed demand for southern journalists from the New York magazines, that we were paid well in real money for our articles and then our stories, and we were so damn happy for it, for we were poor, tired, frustrated, and maniacally ambitious. She knew that writing doesn't flourish in the South because we swap stories on the porch. She had little patience with mythologies. She knew that one opportunity led to another, that writers like Welty and Faulkner developed critical minds that allowed them to be of this place and not of this place at the same time. And she knew that the greatest fiction of this place has been written by people who are so incredibly daring that they are willing to cast a critical eye on its values and customs while standing in the very center of it.

Jeanne and I spoke about her plans for *The Other Side of Air* almost daily, from its inception to the week before her death. We often passed sentences, passages, and chapters of our current work back and forth, generally more for encouragement than commentary. It was not difficult to see when her grief began overwhelming her—I could see it in her words, in the tone, and in what seemed to be a growing inability to set her thoughts in order. She knew literature expertly enough to know how hard a task she had set for herself under the most benign circumstances, and she was fighting on two fronts—one real, in her silent home; and one in this imaginative place she had created. What I have done in this book is to try to make Jeanne's second novel into the one she so carefully described to me before the chaos she contended with on a daily basis took over and made it impossible for her to manage both of her worlds at once. If I never do another literary thing in my life, to have let my friend live on through her beloved imaginative world and in her readers' imagination will, simply put, be good enough. It is important for me to say that Jeanne did not abandon the novel, but had she laid it aside until her turmoil had passed, she still would have had the support and guidance of her agent and editor, who were important to her beyond measure, though no one was enough, nor were they going to be enough. We are all still shocked, and vastly aggrieved.

If there is any lesson to be learned through the death of a writer as dear, as brave, and as brilliant as Jeanne Braselton, it may have something to do with observation and gratitude. Jeanne loved being a writer, and by that I do not mean anything crass. I do not mean to imply that she gloried in having gained access to any kind of special or chosen group. Rather, she loved using the language of her place, of Georgia, to both document and transcend the life of that place. This is a gift she was given that she nurtured and was on her way to exploiting to its fullest benefit, not just to herself but to thousands of readers. If I were to ask her tonight—and there are not many nights when I feel as though I am not asking her—what she would have any of us learn from her death, I am certain that she would tell us to be more alert to the world around us, to the people in line with you at the grocery store, to strangers on the street. She would tell us to look and to listen to the whole flawed lot of them. And she would say, I am evermore sure, to be careful to remember that we all have a story, and each one is a dear, dear thing, waiting to be told in our own words and in our own ways, but always with love and with the terrific stillness of Joy.

Raleigh, North Carolina
September 2005

READING GROUP
Questions and Topics for Discussion

1. *The Other Side of Air* begins, "Now that I have died, I see all and know all." How is opening the book in the voice of a dead narrator a powerful narrative technique? Does it force you to suspend disbelief? How?

2. As a reader, what do you learn immediately about the narrator Katy and her personality, her family, and what she finds most important in life (and death)? What do you find most compelling about her character?

3. What characteristics does Rose possess that makes her the "right company for Ephraim," in Katy's eyes? Why does Ephraim eventually accept her into his life? Why do Ann and Wyatt do so after their initial objections?

4. Before her death, Katy muses about "how little permission sacrifice had brought" in her relationship with Wyatt. What sacrifices did Katy and Ephraim make for Wyatt? What do you think they were seeking in return from their son? Did Wyatt make any sacrifices for them?

5. Wyatt's relationship with his parents is a contentious one. What about his personality does not jibe with his mother and father? Why do you think Ephraim labels his son "unkind"? Do you think this assessment is accurate?

6. Why do you think Wyatt considered himself excluded from his parents? Do you think his parents could have included him more in their lives? How does Wyatt's childhood resentment bubble over into his relationship with his wife, Ann?

7. Katy remarks that Ephraim "had always been in extraordinary spiritual condition" (p. 35). Do you agree or disagree? How does Ephraim express his spirituality, and how does that spirituality differ from the spirituality of his wife, his son, and others around him? Why doesn't Ephraim pay as much attention to his physical condition as he does to his spiritual one?

8. How does money influence Wyatt's perception of his parents, both while he is growing up and later on, when they become more affluent? How does the perception of class affect Wyatt, and also his parents before him? What does affluence mean to him and to Ann, whose parents have warned that "she wouldn't inherit a dime if she allowed them to decline and die without their favorite daughter near them in Florida" (p. 45)?

9. How does Braselton paint death in the scenes where Katy and then Ephraim perish? What emotions does she evoke in you, the reader, during those pivotal moments? After reading the afterword, what do you think might have been going through Braselton's mind as she crafted those scenes?

10. Why does Ephraim refuse to help with housework or the everyday duties of home life? How does Katy come to accept this? If you were in her position, how might you react?

11. "I don't know that he'll ever easily put his arms around a pleasure," muses Katy about Wyatt (p. 70). Do you think that Wyatt has begun to change by the end of the novel? How do you think having a child of his own will affect his mindset and behavior?

12. Letters pepper the book—Katy's to Rose, Katy's mother's to Katy, Ephraim's to Wyatt. How are these letters an effective way to move the story forward and to give you, the reader, a better sense

about those who have written those missives? What effect do the letters have on their recipients?

13. Compare and contrast Wyatt's marriage with that of his parents. How do you think Ann might like him to be more similar to his father, as a husband and, perhaps, as a father? How does Wyatt and Ann's modern marriage have some very traditional problems?

14. Why do Ephraim and Ann want Wyatt to surprise them? Do you think his subsequent surprise is a successful one? Why or why not?

15. Why does Katy, and then Rose, suggest that Wyatt buy Ann a corsage? Why do you think Ann is so thrilled with this gift?

16. Katy and her mother believe that "infinity is made only of the chief emotions we felt in life" (p. 127). What are the chief emotions that Katy feels in her life, that she subsequently feels after her death? What emotions do you think Ephraim will feel?

17. What is Ephraim's first reaction to Katy's death? Why do you think he is able to immediately sleep? Why do you think he subsequently measures his life in "how long I'll be made to stay, not how little I have left" (p. 62)?

18. Katy remarks to Wyatt how Flannery O'Connor was capable of observing "with a kind of critical distance" (p. 129). How is this similar to or different from her own relationship with Wyatt, both before and after her death?

19. What do you think the title *The Other Side of Air* means? Did you have a different understanding of the novel's title upon reaching the book's conclusion?

ABOUT THE AUTHOR

JEANNE BRASELTON was born and raised in Georgia. While working as a journalist for the *Rome News Tribune*, she won numerous Georgia Press Association awards. In 2000, she was chosen as one of ten emerging writers at Vanderbilt University's Millennial Gathering of Writers of the New South. Her debut novel, *A False Sense of Well Being*, won the Georgia Author of the Year Award for First Novel and was named one of the top ten first novels of 2001 by *Booklist*. Upon Braselton's untimely death in 2003, her close friend Kaye Gibbons agreed to complete her unfinished second novel, *The Other Side of Air*.